Sexual Intercourse

Rose Boyt was born in 1958.
She lives in London
and is working on her third novel.

ROSE BOYT

Sexual Intercourse

Minerva

A Minerva Paperback

SEXUAL INTERCOURSE

First published 1989
by Jonathan Cape Ltd
This Minerva edition published 1990
by Mandarin Paperbacks
Michelin House, 81 Fulham Road, London SW3 6RB

Minerva is an imprint of the Octopus Publishing Group

Copyright © 1989 by Rose Boyt

A CIP catalogue record for this book
is available from the British Library
ISBN 0 7493 9073 5

Printed in Great Britain
by Cox & Wyman Ltd, Reading

to my mother and my father

One

'Black is so dreary,' said Sylvia. 'Those dahlias,' she said. 'You know that they cross-breed them. They weed out the mutants and the variations. They won't leave nothing alone. Like plastic, ugly they are. Perfect.'

The mourners shuffled into the crematorium. Sylvia adjusted the black head-scarf that was tied firmly under her chin. 'Come along, Norman,' she said, and took his arm.

They made their way out of the sunshine into the building. Sylvia leant on her son. 'Norman,' she hissed in his ear. 'You look gorgeous in that suit.'

Norman winked at her. The crematorium chapel was filling up. Thin strains of a piped tune could be heard emanating from behind an orange curtain that hung at the far end of the chapel. They took their seats.

'Sad really,' said Sylvia. 'Only a vague relation, a distant relative, through marriage, but still . . . makes you think.'

'Ashes to ashes, dust to dust,' said the vicar.

The orange curtain opened and the coffin glided away into the darkness.

Outside in the gardens the mourners dabbed at their

eyes and exchanged condolences. Sylvia wandered on the lawn with her son. They knew no one.

'This lot could be our relations,' said Sylvia.

'I hope not,' said Norman.

Then Sylvia recognised someone. 'It's that girl from the blue house. She looks just like you Norman.'

'Me with tits,' he said, and laughed.

The girl waved at them.

'She's coming over,' said Norman.

The girl was dressed in black clothes that were too small for her.

'She's wearing her old school uniform,' whispered Sylvia.

The buttons of the cardigan were straining across the girl's chest and her skirt was short and worn.

'Hello, I'm Isobel.'

'Hello, dear,' said Sylvia. 'A distant relative,' she added, waving her hand in the direction of the crematorium.

'Oh,' said Isobel. 'She was my second cousin twice removed or something.'

'We must be related then,' said Norman.

'How nice,' said Sylvia. 'And neighbours.'

Two

The sun was still shining in a cloudless sky when Sylvia and Norman reached the blue house where Isobel lived with her father, and hesitated, peering through dismal foliage at the painted plasterwork stuck beneath the first floor windows to the frontage of solid brick. Norman stooped, to avoid catching his hair in the splayed branches of a bush, and pulled a face at his mother. The front door was ornamented with mottled brass-ware and the grimy windows were closed against the summer.

'Dear, dear me,' he said, and took her elbow.

They crossed the road.

'Home,' said Sylvia.

The scrap of garden in front of their house looked inviting; beside the front door was an elaborate garden-chair with reclining back-rest for Norman's sunbathing and some geraniums in pots.

'The sun's still out,' said Sylvia as she went upstairs to change.

The front room was dusted and polished. The curtains had not been drawn. It was peaceful. Norman removed his suit and shirt and hung them on the back of a chair.

Underneath his trousers he wore a pair of multi-coloured shorts. His legs were tanned and muscular.

'Mother,' he shouted, 'I'm going outside.'

As he lowered himself on to the sun-lounger he heard Sylvia calling him from her bedroom. He could not hear what she was saying but he knew it was nothing important. From under the seat of his chair he pulled out a navy-blue sponge-bag containing suntan oils and creams. It was delicious to smell the geraniums, the hot soil and the fragrant lotions as he smeared his brown body and applied cream to his face and neck. The oil gleamed on the muscles of his chest, arms and thighs. He coated his lips and eyelids carefully.

'Yellow River, Yellow River,' he sang.

When he was well covered he lay back, stretched himself, closed his eyes and kept perfectly still.

'Shall I do your back?' asked Sylvia, standing in the doorway of the house and rousing him from a dream.

'Mmm,' said Norman. 'If you would.'

Sylvia rolled up her sleeves. The backs of her hands were freckled.

'Roll over darling,' she said. 'Roll over and let me get at you.'

Norman turned and revealed his broad brown back to the sun.

'Lovely, lovely,' said Sylvia, and squatted down. She poured a pool of oil on to her son's back and stroked it gently into his skin.

'Give me a good rub mother,' he said.

Sylvia pummelled and squeezed. Her breath whined in her chest with the effort of rubbing and Norman groaned.

'All right,' he said. 'All right. That's enough.'

Sylvia smiled and sighed.

'Thanks, mother,' said Norman.

She heaved herself to her feet and her joints cracked. 'There's a good boy,' she said, ambling off into the house. 'I'll fetch you a cold drink.'

Norman lay with his face buried in a cushion and felt the sun heating his back. 'Later, mother,' he said, enjoying himself.

Sylvia rubbed her hands together and their dry backs soaked up the oil. She wiped her palms on her apron and eased herself into a chair. It was pleasant to sit in the gloom of the front room while Norman basked in the sun. It was restful to snatch half an hour with her feet up, before she began to prepare the lunch, in the peace and quiet of the empty house. This half an hour she reserved for herself with her eyes closed and her slippered feet resting on a pouffe. After lunch they would drink a cup of tea together at the kitchen table, and then the housework would begin. Upstairs wanted a good going over. The breath eased gently in and out of her mouth. This was taking the weight off her feet. After the housework it would be time to do the ironing. She would damp down the clothes in the ironing basket and begin the loving smoothing of Norman's shirts, shorts and slacks. For herself she would press five overalls, a clean one for each day of the week. The clothes she wore to work underneath these overalls were drip-dry. So convenient. And what to prepare for lunch? Norman did not like to eat a roast dinner if the weather was nice enough to sunbathe. It would be salad – egg salad, cheese salad, cold chicken salad, ham salad – any salad he fancied. Sylvia would make a mayonnaise for him and boil some new potatoes. Ice-cream for dessert, or tinned peaches. Or both. Lovely. She smiled and began to snore quietly while Norman slept in the sun.

'Mother,' said Norman, 'I'm hungry.'

Sylvia opened her eyes and saw the tanned face and chest of her son above her.

'Ooh Norman, I must have been asleep,' she said. 'I must have dropped off. It's the heat.'

'What's for lunch?' Norman asked. 'I fancy a salad. A nice ham salad.'

'Good,' said Sylvia.

An enamelled saucepan of potatoes was boiling on the stove and the air of the kitchen was thick. Sylvia washed some lettuce and tomatoes in a colander under the tap and wiped them dry with kitchen-paper. On two plates set out on the side-board rolled slices of pink ham were arranged beside halved hard-boiled eggs, the yolks grey-yellow, the whites grey-white. Inside the outer leaves of the lettuce the heart nestled tenderly. Sylvia unfurled the leaves and laid them out. She beat oil and eggs together in a bowl. One yolk had a red eye. Sylvia removed it with her finger and dabbed it off on a paper towel. The oil and yolks became pale.

'Lunchtime,' she called.

They sat together at the table in the steamy kitchen.

'Shall I open the window?' Sylvia asked.

'No,' said Norman. 'Leave it. Eat up. It's nice and warm in here. Is there any mustard?'

'I'll fetch it,' said Sylvia.

'Thanks mother. Delicious mayonnaise. Superb,' he said. 'Bravo.'

'Don't be daft,' said Sylvia.

Norman, blue-eyed and bare-chested, forked his food into his mouth. 'Salad is good for you,' he said. 'Look at my chest. Thirty-two years of age. Not an inch of flab or fat. Slender as a boy.' He laughed.

'Lovely. Slender as a boy,' said Sylvia.

'You are not too bad yourself, mother,' said Norman.

'No, son, I'm not too bad. Apart from my legs. But what can you expect at my age?'

'At your age? Do me a favour.'

'It's the funeral,' she said. 'Makes me think of dying.'

'Don't,' said Norman.

'My hair is so thin,' she said.

'Don't go on, mother.'

'You're a good boy,' said Sylvia.

'Am I mother? Buy me a packet of cigarettes then.'

'Must I? It won't do you any good.'

'Oh go on. Don't be a silly old cow. I'll do the washing-up,' said Norman. He rose from the table and tied a blue-flowered apron round his middle. 'Yellow River, Yellow River,' he sang as he held the smeared plates under the tap.

'See you in a minute,' said Sylvia, and went out.

The geraniums beside the front door were losing their petals; white and red petals drifted away, leaving naked stamens. Norman lay down on the sun-lounger. The hairs of his thighs were golden and the sun was golden behind his closed eyelids. He heard Sylvia calling to him as she returned from the shop.

'What a lovely day,' she called. 'What a lovely breeze.'

Norman opened his eyes and saw his mother moving towards him through the garden. She knelt beside him and laid the packet of cigarettes on his chest. The packet was warm from the sun and from the heat of his mother's hands.

'Thank you, mother,' he said.

Sylvia bent and kissed him on the forehead.

A hot wind stirred the leaves of the plane tree and the patchy trunk shimmered. Norman lit a cigarette, held the inhaled smoke in his chest, and squeezed it out through flared nostrils. The smoke poured out in two ribbons that frayed and twisted together in the air. He blew a smoke-ring, stabbed at it with his finger and stubbed out the cigarette in a flowerpot. Then he roared and leapt to his feet. The sinews of his neck quivered and a solid ridge of oiled muscle hardened across his chest, rising and falling as he moved his arms above his head. He dropped to a crouch, straightened and crouched again. The strain compressed his lips as he stretched to take the weight of his body on his arms and toes. Norman performed one hundred press-ups. The hot wind lifted dust from the earth and dispersed it in the air. The sky darkened and it began to rain.

The girl from the blue house passed by wearing her funeral clothes and holding a black umbrella. Her head was bent against the rain and her eyes were lowered as if she were afraid to raise them. Norman saw that the elbows of her cardigan were threadbare.

'Isobel,' he called out to her.

Perhaps his voice was drowned by the rain; she did not acknowledge his greeting. Inside the black cardigan her shoulders were thin. Her hair was scraped back off her face and fastened at the nape of her neck with a rubber band.

'Hello,' Norman shouted.

Isobel continued to walk in the rain beneath her black umbrella. It was important to her to retain the even looseness of her stride because to falter or to stiffen would be to give herself away. The man with the naked chest, glistening with oil, streaming with water, was shouting at her. She had seen him oil himself after lunch and kiss the earth one hundred times. The knuckles of his toes had whitened. To adjust the level of her chin, blink, or run her tongue across her teeth would be to acknowledge him. Her teeth were stuck to her upper lip. She wanted him to see that she did not see him. In order to stop herself from blushing she thought of the funeral. She concentrated on the death of her distant cousin so that her cheeks would remain pale. The tanned man was looking at her. Isobel turned her back on him as she reached the gate to the front garden of the blue house and a hectic patch appeared on each cheek. The tanned man could not see her now.

Three

Isobel folded her umbrella and stuck it in the hall-stand. The scent of her father's pipe smoke was cloying. The embossed wallpaper was saturated with his smell and took its colour from his tobacco. His overcoat was hanging on its peg. Isobel mounted the stairs.

The door of his study was closed. She knocked firmly but there was no answer so she waited, knocked again and entered.

'Father.'

Behind the desk at the far end of the room sat Antony Lord, hiding behind a newspaper. The room was full of books and papers.

'Father.'

The man lowered his newspaper and raised his eyebrows at his daughter, making a long, rising, interrogative noise in his throat.

'Would you like a cup of tea?'

Antony Lord did not look at his daughter – his eyes were fixed in space above her head. The newspaper rustled as he raised it again. Then he grunted.

'Father.'

He lowered his newspaper and closed his eyes in boredom. 'What?'

'Nothing,' said Isobel. 'I'll bring you some tea.'

'Thank you,' he said, and yawned.

The kitchen window was streaked with rain and sunshine. Isobel put the kettle on, spread a clean white cloth on the tray and laid out the china. From a slab of fruit cake wrapped in greaseproof paper she cut two slices for her father's tea. On the window-sill a few flowers bloomed in a glass jar. When the kettle boiled Isobel made tea, put the flowers on the tray beside the teapot, and mounted the stairs.

Isobel shifted the tea tray on to one palm and balanced it while fumbling with the study door knob. She steadied the tray against her chest as it slipped, and tried again to open the door. The handle was stiff. The pressure needed to open it might spill the milk in its small white jug or scatter cake crumbs onto the carpet. Isobel's father sat at his desk, watched the door knob, and listened to his teaspoon on the tray rattling against his cup and saucer. Isobel knew that he would not open the door for her so she put the tray down on the floor and used both hands to turn the knob.

'Hello,' said Isobel, as she stood in the doorway holding the tray.

Antony looked up at his daughter. 'Isobel,' he said. 'You did not knock.'

'I'm sorry,' she said. 'Here's your tea. I've brought you your tea.'

Antony glanced at the tray and made a gesture with his hand. 'Put it here,' he said.

His desk was stacked with notebooks and manuscripts. Isobel put the tray on the floor and picked up a pile of magazines from the desk.

'What on earth are you doing?' said Antony.

'Clearing a space for the tray.'

'I must ask you never to touch my work,' said Antony.

'I think I have mentioned this to you before. My work must never take second place to matters of domestic convenience. Please leave me.'

Isobel stood awkwardly holding the pile of magazines and looked down at her feet. 'I brought you some flowers,' she said.

Her father was writing rapidly in the margin of a book. 'What?' he asked absently.

'I brought you some tea and cake and flowers.'

Without raising his head her father said 'Go away.'

Isobel replaced the magazines and shuffled out of the room, closing the door gently behind her. She stood on the landing and listened.

Through the skylight above her the bathed and trembling leaves of a tree shone in the brightness pouring out of the sky. The rain was no longer falling. Isobel's head began to ache with waiting for noises to interrupt the stillness behind the door of the study. Perhaps the tanned man was sunbathing. She opened the door of her own room and reached behind the curtains for the binoculars she kept hidden in an old needlework bag. Squatting down at the window she focused the lenses on Norman.

Curled up on his side, with one arm cradling his head, the man appeared to be asleep in his own embrace. In sleep his mouth was loose and fat. There was a soft sleepy fidget as he rolled over; his face was blurred as he slid his hand inside the front of his shorts. Norman's mother appeared at the front door and stood in the garden looking at her son. The woman shook her head and pressed her lips together as if she knew she was being watched. Isobel heard her father's step outside her door and hid the binoculars.

'May I come in?' said Antony.

'Yes,' she replied.

His presence in her room made Isobel see through his eyes. The small bed, draped with a crumpled white cover, looked suddenly narrow and mean, soiled like the bed of a child. Her coloured rug seemed brash and messy beneath her father's feet; he kicked the rug up thoughtlessly into ridges and raised dust. A pair of her shoes, newly polished and shining, looked ridiculous perched side by side on a chair. Underclothes were heaped on the table in a tangle of greying pink nylon and elastic. Isobel saw that they were frayed and unclean.

Her father turned to face her and spoke. 'Your complexion is very fresh,' he said.

'Thank you,' said Isobel.

They stood awkwardly beside the window. Antony glanced out towards Norman and his mother in their little garden and looked away.

'Do you know those people?' Isobel asked. 'Apparently we're distant cousins or something.'

'I should think not,' Antony replied, and walked out of the room.

At dusk the street was drying; a translucent blueness gathered above the tarmac and pavements, lending a strange luminescence to the house before the shadows thickened and the blueness became opaque. Isobel sat at the window of her room and breathed the sweetness of the drying street. She wept, overcome by dreariness, and then her tears evaporated, leaving behind them a swollen itchiness that made her sigh; the soreness of her eyes pricked her, as she sat on a stool twisting her legs together, with a vision of her death by drowning, in a vale of her own tears.

I am thin. I am delicate. I am sad. Is that a vein or artery showing blue on the underside of my wrist? What a pity. What a pity. She caressed the downy hollow between her nose and upper lip. The compression of the little hairs was minute and pleasing. My father wears a beard. His beard is dark and neatly trimmed. The moustache would overhang if untended. The edge of the beard is a precise line under the lower lip. Between the line and the lip there is a thin edge of bluish skin. The red mouth is rude in the hole in the beard. A kiss without a moustache is like an egg without salt. That is one of his sayings. Not that he ever kisses me. Not even goodnight not since I was seven. What about when he eats hard-boiled eggs and some yolk is trapped in his moustache? My father is so unnoticing. He does not notice those people whose geraniums stand as sentry on either side of their front door. He does not know their smart garden furniture or their multi-coloured underwear. He would not condescend: he is not interested: perhaps he is afraid. Isobel heard the furious rattle of his typewriter. Antony Lord translated articles and pamphlets and wrote pieces for small magazines. The tanned man lived with his mother and did nothing all summer but sunbathe and train. What was he training for? Isobel was pestered by a nagging curiosity. She remembered the voluptuous chubbiness of Norman's sleeping mouth and looked out of the window. At that moment the front door of his house opened. There was Norman on the doorstep in pyjamas and a paisley dressing-gown. The light from the carriage-lamp beside the door bathed his head in a yellowish glow like a halo. He surveyed his garden and the street beyond as if he were looking for somebody. Isobel saw from behind the curtain that he was looking up at her window.

Norman passed a hand over his forehead and whistled a brief melody. The tune was melancholy. Isobel snorted to herself; the man was absurd.

In the fridge there was a jar of rollmop herrings, a box of cakes and some potato salad in a lidded polystyrene container. Isobel descended the stairs noisily to annoy her father, and ate straight from the fridge. She used her fingernail to cut the Sellotape of the unopened box of cakes and carried two chocolate éclairs upstairs surreptitiously to eat in bed.

At last, in spite of her furred teeth and the light of the bedside lamp shining through her eyelids, she went to sleep. Her sleep was dreamless.

Four

When she woke up Isobel was glad it was morning. The sun would bring Norman out in his underpants. She tumbled out of bed and looked out of the window. Norman was lying flat on his stomach, his arms and legs splayed out on the small patch of grass beside the garden path. She wanted to speak to him. It was so boring hanging about in the house. At least Norman was human. Isobel got dressed.

The need to buy a pint of milk was a pretext for passing slowly down the street in the sunshine. The dress she wore was sleeveless and well-cut. Her hair was loose. The idea was to look beautiful yet casual. Isobel was not sure whether she was beautiful or not. She thought she could be said to be attractive.

Anyway Norman was sure to notice her. She left the pavement outside her house and began to cross the road diagonally, intending to reach the other side just before she passed Norman's gate. Isobel swung her arms and flicked her hair back with two fingers. Some children appeared suddenly on bicycles; she faltered, swerving to let them pass, mounted the pavement right in front of Norman's gate, and averted her eyes to avoid his. Passing slowly she waited for him to call out; she prolonged the opportunity for him to greet her by hesitating to bend and adjust the strap of her sandal; she slipped her finger between the leather and the skin. Norman did not call out to her. Perhaps he was asleep.

Under the green awning of the corner shop a woman bent to search for a sound onion in a sack. Flies, sleepy and bloated, fed on pyramids of rotting fruit. The dark shop smelled of salt fish. Isobel inspected the items on the shelves, peering at jars of strange preserves and lingering over the bucket of pink pigs' tails in red pickle that stood at the back on the floor by the paraffin dispenser. She wanted to give Norman time to stir in his sleep and wake up, so that when she walked by on her way home he would call out to her. She picked up a pint of milk and a tin of anchovies in olive oil. Behind the cash register the sullen shopkeeper sighed as he weighed and wrapped an onion. His stomach hung over his belt and rested on his thighs. One by one he dropped the coppers handed to him into the till.

'Good morning,' he said to Isobel.

'Good morning,' she replied.

'The rain,' he said.

'Mmm,' said Isobel. 'Terrible.'

The man looked her up and down. 'Not good for business,' he said. 'Not good at all.'

Isobel could think of nothing to say. She paid the shopkeeper and made for the door.

'Thank you young lady,' he said.

She turned and smiled at him. He was fat and ugly and smelled of fish but still she smiled. And now for Norman.

Inside a plastic bag the wet carton of milk and the tin of anchovies packed in yellow cardboard swung against Isobel's legs. The corner of the milk carton jabbed her in the shin so she lifted the bag and clutched it across her chest. This was awkward; her breasts were squashed, the skin of the encumbered forearm was reddened, and one arm dangled. Isobel considered discarding the shopping, dumping it in a lidless bin that stood in the gutter or flinging it coolly over a bush into a flower bed. Was milk leaking through the bag on to her dress? She lowered her eyes to inspect it. The cloth was creased but not soiled. With her free arm she rearranged the bag between her breasts and looked up. Norman was approaching along the sunny pavement. She dropped the shopping and caught it again as it slid down her body. Norman bounded towards her.

'Hello, hello,' he called.

Isobel exhaled until her chest was empty. Her head was empty.

The legs of Norman's shorts fluttered. 'Hello,' said Isobel.

Norman held out his hands to receive the carton of milk and the tin of anchovies balanced precariously against Isobel's stomach.

'Allow me,' he said, taking them easily in one hand. 'I'm going for a walk,' said Norman. 'My mother is at work. Coming?' he asked.

'All right,' said Isobel. 'I will.' Her insides gurgled audibly. 'Excuse me,' she said.

'Excuse you, what for?' said Norman.

It was clear that he had not heard the intestinal noise. Or perhaps he was too polite to acknowledge it.

'Nothing,' she said, and blushed.

Isobel turned to follow Norman past the shop into streets where all the houses were dingy. Behind shabby palings that smelled of creosote the privet was tall and unkempt. A dirty escarpment slid into railwayland. Chicken-wire divided the land into allotments where cabbages had gone to seed. A train passed, its windows glinting. Hoardings, bearing faded posters, rose out of the scrub and bramble on stilts. There was a smell of cabbage.

'Cabbage,' said Norman.

'Yes,' said Isobel.

'Are you on holiday?' Norman asked as they walked side by side into the park.

'I'm going to university in October,' Isobel replied.

'Oh,' said Norman. 'I see.'

'Are you?' Isobel asked.

'Am I what?'

'Are you on holiday?'

'Yes.'

'What do you do?'

'Not much.'

'What do you want to do?'

'Nothing,' said Norman. 'I like being at home.'

The enormity of time available to a man who lived at home and did nothing stretched out before Isobel. He had time enough for himself and perhaps for her.

'Don't you want to do anything?' Isobel asked.

'Not particularly.'

'No plans?'

'No, no plans. Have you got plans then?' asked Norman.

'I suppose so,' she said. Her own plans were laid out rigidly before her. 'I need plans,' she said.

'Why?'

'I don't know. I need them.'

'I don't,' said Norman.

'Oh I do.'

'So you said.'

Norman extended one finger and touched Isobel on the neck. 'What do you want to be?' he asked.

'I don't know,' said Isobel. 'Aren't you afraid of dying?'

'It's the funeral,' said Norman. 'Getting you down.'

'No,' said Isobel. 'But aren't you afraid of dying?'

'No.'

A stillness was contained in green shadows between the trunks of old trees. Above them, caught in leafy canopies, the sunshine was yellow.

'What about famous last words?' said Isobel.

'What about them?'

'Don't you worry about them?'

'Whose?'

'Yours.'

'No. Do you?'

'Yes. I hope I die in my sleep. It gives me the horrors to think of myself laid out on my death bed as if I were dead already staring at the ceiling and trying to think of something to say. I might start screaming. I know I won't be ready. How will I resign myself? What if I have wasted my life?'

'Well don't then,' said Norman, and lit a cigarette.

'What about you?' she asked.

'What about me? I told you. I don't care. It doesn't bother me.'

Isobel looked into his calmly smiling face and saw that he was not afraid. In fact he was grinning.

'You could say "I have lived life to the full" and close your eyes with a smile of satisfied resignation and die nobly or you could die defiantly with your eyes open shouting "I look death in the face" or you could die beautifully whispering to Christ with longing in your voice. The choice is yours.'

'Oh shut up,' said Isobel. 'You know what I mean.'

'Yes,' said Norman. 'As a matter of fact I do.'

They sat down together on the grass. The park was deserted.

'What is your middle name?' Isobel asked.

'My middle name is Augustus. Norman Augustus Brake.'

'A mouthful,' said Isobel. 'I haven't got a middle name.'

'Lucky,' said Norman. 'My father chose mine. According to mother he was ever such an educated person. According to mother that's where I get my brains from. "Love 'im," she says. Silly old cow. She hasn't seen him for thirty years. Still, she's a good woman, my mother,' said Norman.

'Let's go home,' said Isobel.

Outside the park gates a small pony stood harnessed to a cart. Its eyes were filmy and clouded behind pale lashes and long whiskers grew out of indented follicles in the rubbery lip. The coat of the animal was dusty, and its teeth, yellow and enormous, were bedded in pink gums. It waited between traces without stamping, and chewed.

In the shade of his awning, the man from the corner shop folded his arms across his flabby chest and surveyed his merchandise.

'Afternoon,' he called out as Isobel and Norman walked past him.

'All right?' Norman replied.

Isobel smiled.

'I'll slip off now,' said Norman, as they approached his house. Sylvia was watering the geraniums. 'See you later,' he said, and pushed open the gate.

The gate clattered. Isobel was left alone on the pavement, hesitating and flushed. She began to swing her stiff arms as she set off across the road and remembered – Norman was carrying her shopping. Foolishly she continued towards the blue house, empty-handed.

At the curb Isobel turned just as Norman followed his mother into the hall of their house and pulled the door shut behind him. To return to the shop for more milk would be simpler than ringing Norman's polished doorbell and waiting on the scrubbed step as the chimes vibrated into the quiet afternoon, but the thought of the shopkeeper's fat face smiling at her knowingly made her feel sick. She hurried home.

Empty coats, worn out or out-grown and hanging for years in the dark hallway gave off dust as she passed. A faint urinal aroma rose from a rubberised mackintosh. Isobel heard the knock of knuckles on the front door and gasped. The shaggy head of her father appeared over the banisters. Isobel saw up his nose.

'Well answer the door dear,' he said, his voice controlled to disguise keenness.

Isobel opened the door.

'Hello there,' said Sylvia. 'You left these things in the

shop,' she said, handing over the carton of milk and the tin of anchovies. Isobel saw her wink.

'Oh thank you so much.'

Sylvia peered into the hall and raised her eyes just in time to catch a glimpse of the great bearded head of Antony Lord as it disappeared. 'Your father?' she whispered at Isobel.

'Yes.'

Sylvia smiled broadly. The breath she pushed out of her strapping chest sounded through her teeth like a sigh of pity, or a whistle of disgust. 'Why not pop over for tea Tuesday?' she said.

'Thank you, I will.'

Waving enthusiastically the woman withdrew and loped across the street. Isobel closed the front door.

'Who was that woman?' Antony Lord was shouting as he descended the stairs. 'What did she want? Why was she talking to you? Where have you been all day?' He stepped neatly off the last stair and joined his daughter in the hall. 'Well?' he demanded. A film of sweat coated his brow. He held two plump white hands out palm upwards as if in readiness to receive an answer. Isobel placed the milk carton in one of his hands and took the other gently in her own.

'I've been out for a walk,' she said.

'Why are you holding my hand?' Antony asked.

'Why not,' said Isobel, pressing his wrist with her thumb. 'Would you like something to eat?'

He mumbled as she led him into the kitchen. Their hands slipped apart.

'What did you say Dad?'

'Nothing.'

Antony sat down at the kitchen table and stroked his bearded chin. 'By the way, who was that woman?' he asked.

'You know,' said Isobel. 'The one that lives over the road. Sylvia. From the funeral. I left the milk in the shop.'

'Oh her,' said Antony, blinking. 'Forget the sandwich,'

he said, stumbling to his feet and out of the kitchen.

Isobel heard the shuffling of her father's feet as he climbed the stairs. His beard was threaded through with whitish or pale yellow hairs.

'Silly sod,' Isobel mouthed. 'Miserable old bastard.'

Five

In the middle of the night a scream dragged Isobel out of her bed. It was the rasp of floorboards on the soles of her feet that woke her.

The cry was repeated. Her father was calling for her – 'Isobel, Isobel.'

A loose board squealed. Entering her father's bedroom she made out, swathed in blankets, his humped form rocking on the bed. Rocking he butted his hairy head against the headboard, turned his head sideways and showed a white cheek; his mouth bit out a gash in his beard; rocking he cried out – 'Isobel, Isobel.'

Isobel embraced her father's head. She folded it in her arms and whispered to him. The puckered eyes and slack mouth gave off moisture that coated her dry fingers. His beard was wet. Her father was moaning. She caressed him and his head became still and quiet in her hands. He turned in his bed and Isobel loosened her hold on him. His cheek was beached on the pillow, an eye opened in its wet socket, and the slack mouth contracted. Antony woke up in the arms of his daughter and screamed. 'Get out of my room you stupid child.'

The hairy face was split open showing teeth and shining gums momentarily before it jerked away and buried itself in the bed. A muffled voice could be heard under the covers. Isobel, wrapping her arms round her own chest and crying silently, left her father and returned to her own bed.

The wait for the dawn was a nasty vigil. The sheets were crumpled and crumbed with grit from the floor that had clung to Isobel's feet; morsels of food, dropped from her mouth or plate during other lengthy stays in bed, had lodged themselves in the folds of the bedding; creases had been sweated in and dried out, pressed by the weight of her sleeping body. She watched the blackness of the sky out of the window, nudged a rounded fist into a sleepy eye, and waited for the greying of morning.

I am not going to get up. There is a bucket under the bed, rimmed with lime scale, smelling of disinfectant, that I will piss in when I need to piss, or shit in, and puke.

Beside the bed on a small table stood a jug of stale water, a pile of books and a clock. The blackness of the night was dissolving. A wind swiftly dispersed cloud and the sky became pale. Isobel set the clock by guesswork and settled down to stay in bed. She slept.

The rattling of her father's typewriter fingered her grossly out of a delicate dream; sleep, its embrace prised open, relinquished her; she was taken by pads of hardened fingers pressing to depress keys and shunting the carriage, and opened her eyes. She was not going to get up. The clock said one o'clock. Her father was rattling on regardless. Isobel groped under the bed for the bucket and pissed in it; the urine was bright yellow; she shoved the bucket back under the bed.

Across the mouth of the jug on the bedside table a fine film of dust and small fibres had settled on the surface of the water. Isobel lifted the jug to her lips and gulped the water down. A bitten éclair, left over from Sunday, bore toothmarks in its flabby filling; the sweetened cream was yellowing; a whitish deposit of sweated moisture coated the chocolate. Isobel ate it and licked her fingers. Her father was clattering about in the kitchen. He must have crept downstairs stealthily and now he was making himself some lunch. The smell of toast and frying bacon drifted into her bedroom; she pulled the covers up over her head.

In the dark tent of sheets and blankets the ticking of the clock could not be heard. The smell in the bed was her own smell. Soon she became accustomed to it. She dozed and stirred and dozed and slept and dreamed.

The shrink of time in dreamless sleep was a foretaste of death. Waking she counted out the hours in seconds, one by one: each minute measured against centuries. Dreaming compressed life into a moment; a night of dreams was compacted into a wink. Waiting was hellish – the lurching stretch and shrink of time rattled the plans that Isobel had erected against the future. The emptiness of hunger compounded the hollowness of such thought and her father rattled away regardless.

The telephone was ringing. Isobel heard the scrape of chairlegs on floorboards as her father got up to answer it. His corduroys were limp and worn by much agitated sitting. A red and white blotch of knuckle marks on his cheek faded with the break in contact between his head and his hand.

'Hello,' he shouted into the receiver. 'Hello,' he repeated.

Through the wall Isobel heard him bellowing.

'Hello,' he shouted, abruptly adjusting his indifferent tone to one of huge jollity. 'Oh yes. Marvellous. Please. Yes. Good.' His laughter was rich and fruity. 'Oh yes. Half past seven. Until then. Marvellous.' Antony replaced the receiver and wiped the palm of his hand on the seat of his trousers. Stepping out briskly he began to pace up and down in his study, leaving the ink on the nib of a lidless pen to dry on his desk and a sentence unfinished. Isobel heard his frantic pacing. It was clear that he was not working. Why then did he not come to see her?

Curling up between the sheets Isobel nursed the ache

of loneliness. She could feel, as she stroked herself with nimble fingers, the pitiful poking of ribs through spare flesh. She was terribly empty. What if she died? Then he would be sorry.

A single knock of the knocker pressed firmly to meet the metal stud on the front door silenced the whine of Isobel's loneliness; she sat up and kept very still as her father bounded down the stairs. Neatly the oily click of the lock sprung back in the silence. A woman's yelp of pleasure defined for Isobel the nature of her father's guest. The foolish clatter of heels on linoleum was accompanied by assorted heavy footfalls indicating to Isobel that the woman was not alone.

The silvery kiss of glass on glass punctuated the murmuring of voices in the sitting-room. The woman's laugh spilt from her lips again and again, stamping feet shook the ceiling, and a man's voice repeated the first line of a song. Isobel rested the flat of her hand on her chest and stomach and thighs and a question echoed in her hollow insides – Why doesn't he come to me?

The mad itch of waiting was exacerbated by the woman's laugh. What on earth could be so funny? Isobel's cheeks coloured to think of her father singing or dancing. He must be drunk. The advent of guests, although diminishing the chance of Isobel receiving a visit from her father, alleviated the boredom of waiting. She could tease herself with supposition. She could wound herself with surmise. At least the incessant rattling of her father's fingers on the keys of his typewriter had ceased. This fact made room for the operation of the imagination.

Of course she knew that there was an alternative plan of action open to her. It was possible for her to stop waiting for her father to come to her, his head bowed in submissive guilt, coveting her forgiveness and wheedling for pity, holding out his white hands to her for her embrace, raising hands to his face to hide his shame – she knew that it was possible to stop waiting and go to him. She would rise from her bed in her furled nightgown, her hair matted to the skull, unwashed, unkempt, undressed; she would stand before her wardrobe mirror and remove her nightgown, revealing to herself her pale nakedness, and prepare herself for the surrender of her vigil; she would lacerate the thin skin of her breasts and thighs with the razor blade that lay inside its slim packet in the soap-dish on her bedside table; she would smear blood across her mouth and eyes; she would shear her hair to the blue scalp and screaming as she leapt into the sitting-room where her father was presiding over an orgy or whatever he was doing down there she would bleed and scream – she knew it was possible and yet waiting had made her inert. She would have to wait for him.

Then there were footsteps on the stairs, the tip-toe footsteps of one who had removed her shoes, the quiet pad pad of stockinged feet released from the constriction of high heels, the slip slip of damp nylon catching on the stairs. The woman's thighs brushed together. She must be looking for the bathroom. Of course she did not like to ask Antony; it was more subtle just to slip out and find it for herself. Isobel heard her approaching and turned on the bedside lamp. The unfamiliar step paused outside her bedroom. The door of her room opened.

'Oh, I'm so sorry,' said the woman, raising one hand to her mouth. Isobel assumed an expression of sickly pain. She hoped she bore the near-death pallor of the bedridden. Feigning sleep, bathed in the light of the reading lamp that illuminated her pitiful face, she groaned. The woman shut the door hastily. She would go downstairs and tell Antony and at last he would come. The lavatory was flushing. The woman descended the stairs. Isobel waited, and smiled.

The woman must have said nothing – that was the only bearable explanation. She looked the prudish type. After all it was not as if she would hurry downstairs to Antony and grasp him by the hand and say 'Oh Antony I went upstairs to do a shit but I opened the wrong door and saw a lovely young girl dying in her bed.' As if she would.

The woman was bound to keep quiet. Her stupid manners prevented her from saving Isobel.

The cacophony rising from below was tormenting. Isobel buried her head under the pillow and stuck her fingers in her ears. The noise became more raucous; there was some moving of furniture followed by a period of suspicious quietness. Perhaps the guests had crept away. The quiet was disrupted by a bout of frantic knocking. Again the sound of the woman's laugh combined with the sound of footsteps, and jovial greetings rang out in the hall. 'Hello, hello, hello, hello, hello.' The woman laughed like a clucking chicken. Someone turned on the radio and human sounds were drowned by the squeak of the orchestra. The melody poured into Isobel's ear and she slept.

The night was black and silent. Isobel slipped out of bed and listened at her father's door. The air on the landing was poisoned by the smell of tobacco and scent. She strained her ears outside his bedroom and heard nothing but ugly snoring. Isobel returned to her bed and slept the blank dreamless sleep of grief.

When she woke up in the morning the bucket under her bed was half full of oily urine. The jug of water was empty. Isobel's breath reeked out of her hungry guts. Squatting over the bucket she produced a stream of piss that stirred up a bitter stink. Hunger seized up her bowels and the foul smells she emitted made her resolute; it was time to confront her father. She had waited long enough and now could wait no longer.

Her shaky legs almost gave way beneath her; it was delightful to be weak, to stumble, almost swooning, and sigh. She held out her hands and watched them tremble. The bones in her face protruded and shadows gathered in the sockets of her eyes. There was a glamour in shadows that savoured of death.

To wear black would be funereal. The sad translucent whiteness of her face would shine. Black clothes had a slimming effect. Pale and thin, pale and thin. The smudges under her eyes would look like bruises. And yet to clothe her limp body in white as if she were dead already would make his heart bleed.

The white dress sheathed her lean body and her eyes grew enormous. She was staring at herself in the mirror. He would not be able to resist.

Opening the door of her room Isobel called out – 'Father.' Flinging open the doors of his bedroom and study she repeated the cry. The rooms were empty. She ran downstairs. The sitting-room was empty. The kitchen and the dining-room were empty. Where had he gone?

Isobel steadied herself with one hand on the table and lowered herself into a chair. She hid her face to cover her own foolishness and grimaced. Some melancholy surrender. What a marvellous walking corpse in a shroud.

On the greasy wooden board balanced on top of the fridge was a big white dish holding two chicken carcasses. Isobel had never seen the dish before. One of the guests must have brought it. The carcasses were sunk in a pool of their own stiffened juices. The linked bones of a stripped neck lay grey and chewed on the draining board. Isobel mopped up the jellied juice with bread, salted and peppered the sodden slices, and crammed them into her mouth. The chicken fat coated her fingers and slipped into the gap between her fingertip and fingernail. The yellow fat made her lips shine. Air caught in the parcels of folded bread and went down with them into Isobel's stomach. The fat starch paste adhered to her gums and she loosened it with her tongue as she bent over to open the fridge.

Stacked inside were many packages wrapped in cling-film and tin-foil. The laughing woman must have prepared these things lovingly and brought them over to tempt Antony's feeble appetite. The chickens must have ridden side by side on their dish on the back seat of her car like children. A stuffed pepper with piquant filling fell out of the fridge on to the floor and burst. Isobel ate some of the rice off the lino

and kicked the rest under the sink. The woman could clear
it up. Raising her bare arm to her mouth she wiped away
a moustache of fat and peered guiltily out of the window.
Let him come. Isobel felt sick.

In the dining-room dust shone and spun in dreary sunbeams. The plastic leather seats of the dining chairs made
a bed for Isobel half under the table. She slid herself on to
this unyielding ledge, opened her legs and stuck her hand
into her knickers. Out of the blackness behind her eyes the
bearded image of her father stared impassively, mocking her
desire. She tried to banish her father by thinking of Norman
and made herself come. It was nearly tea time. Isobel licked
her finger clean. It was time to be welcomed into the bosom
of Norman's family. She rose, straightened her skirt, and
crossed the road.

Six

'Hello, dear,' said Sylvia. 'Welcome, welcome, come in.'

The hall was swept and polished. A bunch of carnations stood on a spindly stand in a white vase with a relief freize and two handles, designed in imitation of a Grecian urn. Sylvia led Isobel into the front room where Norman was sitting in an armchair, resting his head against an antimacassar of white lace. 'I'll go and put the kettle on,' she said.

Norman leapt to his feet and shook hands with Isobel across a low table laden with cakes and plates of dainty sandwiches, then dropped her hand cleanly and gestured towards a chair, waiting for her to be seated before resuming his own position. He looked at her with wide eyes. Sylvia returned carrying the teapot and tea was served.

Saucers clicked dully on the tablecloth and small sounds of sipping and chewing rose with excruciating familiarity out of every mouth. The polite little noises filled Isobel with a sense of impending doom, and yet nothing untoward occurred. No one burped or farted. No one screamed or allowed laughter to explode, or fainted. They sat quietly in their armchairs and ate, drank and conversed.

'Norman says you are going to university, dear,' said Sylvia.

'Yes, I am.'

'What will you be learning?'

'Classics,' said Isobel. 'I will be reading classics.'

'Ooh,' said Sylvia. 'Classics. Lovely.' She beamed.

Norman rolled his eyeballs and raised his eyebrows towards the ceiling to show Isobel that he thought his mother was daft.

'Delicious scones,' said Isobel, spreading the split surface with jam and cream.

'Oh thank you so much. Norman loves them. You know Norman has a sweet tooth.'

'Mother!'

'Well you have dear, and its nothing to be ashamed of.'

'Have you got a sweet tooth Norman?' Isobel asked.

Norman said nothing. The two women smiled at each other.

'Come on darling,' said Sylvia. 'Don't sulk. It was only a joke.'

'When I was six I had a sweet tooth. When I was twelve I had a sweet tooth. Now I eat puddings and cakes when they are offered but never instigate their preparation. I only eat them when they are offered. I do not therefore have a sweet tooth,' said Norman.

'I have,' said Isobel.

Norman and Sylvia turned towards her simultaneously and laughed.

'It's different for a woman,' said Norman.

'Okay dear,' said Sylvia. 'We understand, don't we Isobel?'

Isobel stroked the cropped nap of bristling velvet stretched over the arm of her chair; smoothing her forearm across the pile to make it shine and rubbing her forearm against the pile to make it dull she lowered her eyes and said nothing.

'You look pale dear,' said Sylvia.

37

'Me?' said Isobel.

'You do you know.'

'Mother!' said Norman.

'Well she does,' said Sylvia. 'Are you all right?'

'Fine. Yes. I'm fine. Actually I do have a slight headache.'

'You poor dear. Why didn't you say? Let me get you something. It's no good suffering in silence now is it? Open the window Norman, let some air in. Here take this Isobel – that's better.'

'Don't fuss mother,' said Norman.

'It's okay,' said Isobel. 'Thank you. You're so kind.'

The large white pill lodged in her chest. She took a sip of tea and washed it down into her stomach where it dissolved.

'Better dear? Better eh?' Sylvia insisted. 'Why don't you two young people get out into the sunshine and go for a walk?'

'Would you like to?' Norman asked. 'How about it?'

'That would be nice,' said Isobel.

'Isobel,' said Sylvia. 'Isobel, Isobel, Isobel. I can't get used to it. I thought something like Fiona would have suited you better. Fiona or Emma or Rose. Not Isobel. It's not quite you dear – is it? Let's call you Fiona instead dear shall we? You really are more of a Fiona.'

Norman stood up. 'Leave off mother,' he said. 'You are not her mother. It's not up to you what she is called.'

'Call me Fiona if you like,' said Isobel. 'I rather like it.'

'There! See Norman!'

'Come on Isobel,' he said. 'Let's go.'

'Bye bye Fiona,' Sylvia called out after them into the balmy afternoon.

'Mad,' said Norman. 'She's mad.'

'No,' said Isobel.

Then it was straight to the railwayland. A pair of men's shoes, neatly placed side by side at the foot of the fence among weeds, contained water out of which a bloated tongue lolled; the distorted and misshapen leather bore the imprint of a man's feet; the water in the shoes was green. Hollyhocks from windblown seed grew tall and poorly out of the thin soil. Wild camomile scented the air when crushed beneath the feet and brambles drew blood with thorns and painted blood with broken fruit on bare flesh. Nettles and dockleaves grew together. Out of the remains of a shed rose the erect and tumid stems of hogweed nurtured by shelter and defended by menacing spines. Stunted scraps of stalk and bitten leaf grew close to the ground where flints were scattered and in the soil near the dump course grass and iris flourished. An oil drum open to the rain held water teeming with larvae of mosquitoes and the corpses of maggots floating out of a pigeon carcass that had been flung into the drum and sunk. Beside the allotments wasps fed on the sweet fallen fruit of an apple tree.

Isobel was following Norman. 'Where are we going?' she asked.

'Over there.' Norman raised one hand and flapped it vaguely into the distance.

'Where?'

'Not far. I know a nice place to sit down.'

Isobel stepped over an open manhole set in a small square of gravelled concrete. They reached a smashed fence and climbed over. A patch of long grass grew inside the jagged perimeter, bending under the weight of its seeds.

'Here?' asked Isobel, lowering herself awkwardly into the grass.

'Here,' said Norman. 'It used to be a lawn.'

'Yes,' said Isobel, stretching out her slender legs. Norman sat beside her. The grass was warm and made a dusty wall around them.

'Fiona,' said Norman.

They laughed.

Isobel lay back in the grass and squirmed, pressing her ribs and hipbones through the cloth of her dress so that Norman could see how frail she was. She knew that he was watching her. Through meshed lashes Isobel squinted at the sky.

'I might take my clothes off,' said Norman. 'To sunbathe. I've got shorts on underneath.'

Isobel hitched up the skirt of her dress. Beside Norman's brown limbs her thighs were white. They lay side by side in the sunshine. Isobel could hear Norman breathing beside her. She could hear herself breathing. A warm smell emanated from his warmed skin, now masking the grass smell, now masked by it. And with each breath, the urgency of breathing increased; each breath was tighter and sharper than the last. The sun seeped through closed eyelids making a red blindness out of the blue blue sky. They embraced, cradled in redness. The flat of Norman's hand was dry and smooth against the translucent skin of her thighs. He deftly separated them and stuck his brown fingers inside her knickers. They kissed, his tongue fat and agile in her mouth. Isobel's arms closed tightly around him. She held him and felt his hard penis pushing against her. Swiftly he removed her knickers and lowered himself gently onto her. She pulled his shorts down and released his penis from the multi-coloured fabric. She was ready for him.

'Come to me,' she said.

Seven

'How about The George, dear? Do you fancy it? We could walk through the park. I've done the dishes. Or shall we have a cup of tea?' Sylvia was shouting at Norman through the open window of the kitchen.

'I fancy a walk,' said Norman.

'Good.'

Norman remained motionless.

'Get a move on then,' she said.

The washing up water gurgled in the drain. Sylvia was fastening the front of her hair off her temples with a pair of white plastic combs. She examined her reflection in the hall mirror and felt a pair of heavy hands land on the boney width of her hips.

'Ready,' said Norman.

In the mirror she saw his grinning face thrust out playfully from behind her own large head. 'Get off me dear,' she said, and turned, wearily. Suddenly she was tired. The white T-shirt that Norman was wearing set off his tan and his long shorts were made out of an old pair of jeans. 'Very nice,' said Sylvia, with effort, and took his arm.

The grass in the park was dry and warm beneath their feet. In the shade of a dusty plane tree a family had spread themselves on rugs and inflatable lilos. A woman in a red dress knelt on the corner of a table-cloth, serving cake to children; her skin was flayed pink by the sun.

The dust of the baked earth was kicked up by footballers who scuffed bare patches in the grass with their toes as they tackled each other, and skidding gouged out runnels with their heels. The goals were marked out by coloured jerseys, bright against the sapless pitch. On the sidelines groups of women sat and watched.

'Football,' said Norman. 'I like those shorts they wear, those men, look mother. I like those shorts. I really do.'

'Oh Norman,' said Sylvia. 'Don't go on.'

'They are made out of that silky-feel stuff, that shiny stuff – I like it – look!'

'For God's sake Norman,' said Sylvia sourly, pressing each word out between her teeth.

Norman sped away from her across the grass, weaving between the trunks of trees and stroking them in passing as he spun. His eyes were narrow as he careered about the park with his arms outstretched. He found that he was making a small aeroplane noise in his mouth. Through slitted eyes as he spun the solid upright leaning tottering lurching falling figure of his mother wheeled; her lips were pressed together.

'Fuck you,' he bellowed.

Passers-by pointed and stared and looked away. Sylvia shouted at her son as he hurled himself at her out of the trees. To avoid a collision she stumbled out of the way across the yellowing grass. Norman dived to the ground where she had been standing and his face crumpled. Then he began to laugh.

'Get up son,' said Sylvia.

'Bollocks,' said Norman, shaking with laughter as he got to his feet. 'I don't care,' he said.

Sylvia looked at him carefully, her own face held in a resigned and kindly smile.

'Sorry,' he said.

'Come on son,' said Sylvia, taking the hand he held out to her.

They continued to walk hand in hand across the park for a few steps until Sylvia disengaged her hand from Norman's grasp and slid it between his arm and his side.

'That's better,' she said. 'Act your age.'

Norman's face was composed: he adopted a cool and manly stare, closed his mouth firmly and stuck out his chin.

'That's better,' said Sylvia.

A clump of rhododendrons bloomed in the sunshine; the fleshy leaves were dusty and the streaky crimson flowers overblown. A dog worried the roots, digging under bushes for a bone. A path edged with a tiny fence led to the park gates.

'Nearly there,' said Sylvia.

'Are you tired?' asked Norman.

'No, not really.'

'You look it.'

'Thanks.'

'Come on woman,' said Norman.

'Sorry,' she said.

The greetings offered to mother and son as they entered the pub were accompanied by the jangling of coins in the pouched money-belt slung around the middle of the market woman. She bent from the waist to take aim along the pool cue and the satisfying click of ball on ball and the whispering thud of ball on cushion punctuated the sound of raised voices.

'Evening Sylv,' said the potman.

'Hello,' said Mr Green.

'All right Susan?' Maureen called out to her.

'Isn't he lovely,' said Vi.

'Mmm,' said Dolly.

'I seen all sorts in my time,' said Lily. 'Entitled to a bit of fun now and again I am, I reckon.' She reached out with her ringed and stained fingers and touched Norman's thigh as he passed.

'Hello, love,' said Eric. 'What will you be having?'

The juke-box was grinding out a melancholy love song and the fruit machine played an electronic tune.

'A pint of lager for his nibs,' said Sylvia. 'And a lager shandy for myself.'

'Nothing stronger?' asked Eric, leaning across the bar.

'I'll have a dry martini. And lemonade. Live dangerously,' she said, and laughed.

A scuffle broke out by the pool table and attracted some attention. Women's eyes were illuminated by the prospect of a fight. Men rose in their seats and sat down again.

'Hit him Ginger,' Lily shouted and turned to Maureen to continue her conversation.

'Yes dear,' she said. 'I know it was 1960. That was the year his arm was mangled in the sorting machine.'

Mr Green separated the two men.

'And I delivered a baby during the war,' said Lily. 'With my own bare hands.'

Sylvia joined Norman at a table by the window and took a small sip of her drink. Norman's cigarettes were placed beside the ashtray with a box of matches sitting squarely on top.

'Big Ben,' he said, indicating with his eyes across the pub to the gents where a gawping man in a brown suit stood twisting his hands together with his back to the door. 'A shame. Simple,' he added.

'Love 'im,' said Sylvia.

In the shadowy corner by the telephone a man and a woman were talking, their voices harsh with the effort not to be overheard. The man held the woman's upper arm in his bruised hand and shoved his face into hers.

'Give it to me,' he mouthed at her.

44

The woman clutched her purse in her armpit and shook her head.

'Give it to me. I'll die,' said the man.

'Die then,' she said, her face closed against him.

'I love you,' he said. 'I love you. Please.'

The woman opened her mouth to speak and faltered with her mouth open.

'Please,' he said, his eyelids drooping in anticipation.

The woman shook off his hand and took a ten-pound note out of her purse. The man grabbed it and hurried away.

'Junkie,' said Norman.

'It's time you got yourself a little friend,' said Sylvia.

'Why? Are you trying to get rid of me?'

'No, dear, it's not that, it's just that I thought it would be nice for you. Nice for you to get out and live a bit. That Fiona's a nice girl Norman.'

'Yes mother.'

'No, but she is Norman. Just right for you I'd say.'

On the television mounted on a shelf high above the snack counter a street was burning.

'She's called Isobel. Not Fiona,' said Norman.

'It comes to the same thing, dear.'

'Leave me out mother.'

Overhead on the screen, in a blackened wilderness of fire policemen advanced through the smoke carrying shields into a rain of bottles and bricks.

'No really, Norman,' said Sylvia. 'It's about time you settled down.

'I am settled down.'

'You know what I mean.'

'It's the riots on the telly,' said Norman, pointing at the screen.

'Don't change the subject.'

'Poor sods look at them,' said Norman. 'Kill the bastards.'

The battered face of an injured policeman smiling bravely out of a hospital bed appeared on the screen.

'Silly bastard,' said Norman.

'Norman,' said Sylvia. 'I am trying to talk to you.'

'Oh sorry, what about?'

'About you, dear,' she said.

'What about me?'

'You know.'

'What?'

'Forget it,' said Sylvia.

Maureen laughed.

'You are a one,' said Lily, turning the gold hooped earring that hung in the stretched gash in her ear. 'Dirty old cow,' she said.

'Never say die,' said Maureen. 'You're never too old I always say.'

'You should know,' said Violet.

'Charming.'

'Well you said it dear.'

'Come on girls.'

Maureen handed round her cigarettes.

'Have another?' said Dolly, opening her purse and looking into it. 'Same again all round?'

'Thanks,' they said.

Seamus wedged his bulk into the back bar among friends. His clothes were earth-coloured and his eyes were watered with drinking.

'A song Seamus for the love of God,' his friends cried.

Lily raised her glass. 'Here's to him,' she said. 'Compensation? No insurance – the usual story – we settled out of court. Don't get me wrong, poor soul – I wept: set us up lovely. Hello Mr Green. Thank you, I don't mind if I do. Ever such a nice man Mr Green.'

The bar was veneered with wood-grain Formica on which several small towels advertising the brewery were arranged to soak up spilt beer. A small bunch of dahlias, red and mauve, wilted in a cut-glass vase by the ice bucket, and a thin wrought-iron glass rack ran the length of the counter, the glasses gleaming above Eric's head. On the shelf behind him a whole lemon shone on a plate. A small knife lay beside it, the handle made of mother-of-pearl. Above, on a ledge at head height, covered with dusty paper doilies, there was a small bottle of livid cocktail cherries, the lid of which had become greasy with age, a large jar of pickled eggs and an empty giant-sized whisky bottle half full of small change. Eric moved about behind the bar efficiently, in spite of the barmaid's enormous hands. Weaving and flapping about between the sink and the taps and the till, stretching out towards him, smoothing the curve of his buttock, poking him in the softness of his belly or jabbing in between the ribs, her fingers were pointed and dangerous, yet Eric managed to work economically, polishing a glass as he stepped from the sink to the till, opening the lid of a bottle of Babycham as he waited for a pint of Guinness to settle in its glass, catching her gently by the wrist.

'That Mr Green is a very nice man,' said Sylvia, in an innocuous voice.

'Who is Mr Green?'

'You see that gentleman over there?' Sylvia pointed with one finger. 'That one with the little dog?'

'I see,' said Norman. 'Who is he?'

'He is a friend of mine.'

'Why doesn't he come over then?'

'Tact, I suppose, dear.'

'Tact,' Norman repeated, and raised his bitten knuckle to his mouth. 'What do you mean?'

'Well, dear, Mr Green is a very kind and dear friend. He is the last person ever to want to upset you. As my son, that is, you see. He is kind enough not to want to tread on your toes, dear. That's all.'

'Tread on my toes? What do you mean?'

'Oh God Norman, you know.'

'What do I know?'

'Forget it,' said Sylvia, putting her drink down on a circular cardboard beer mat. 'I'm going to the ladies'.' Her face was loose with sadness. She got up heavily, leaving Norman fiddling with his matches.

47

'Cheer up love, it might never happen,' said Lily.

The pint glass in Norman's hand was almost empty and his pockets were empty. The barmaid was standing in front of the juke-box making her selection. The coin dropped and Norman heard the whirring of the mechanism. 'Tie a Yellow Ribbon Round the Old Oak Tree'. The singer of the song was a blind man. And what about Mr Green? Norman glanced at him, caught his eye, and looked away. He looked all right, smiling and harmless, a friendly man. It was nice for his mother to have a friend.

On the television a girl with the sun in her hair was eating a bar of chocolate.

'A penny for your thoughts?' said Sylvia, beaming.

'Nothing, really,' said Norman.

'Not thinking of Fiona, I mean Isobel?'

'No.'

'Oh well, can't be helped I suppose.'

'Get them in,' said Norman.

Sylvia handed him her purse.

'Young people today, I really don't know,' said Dolly.

The bell was ringing. It was time for last orders. It was time to go home.

Eight

Isobel was still in bed. The stale sheets and the long long sunny Sunday were inescapable. To rise demanded an effort of will that Isobel was unable to summon; to sleep until Monday was impossible.

Antony Lord had not returned. Perhaps he was staying in Oxford for a few days to investigate some lesser-known ancient text or had gone abroad to review a foreign film or assess an important exhibition. Perhaps he had gone away, his arm proffered to the woman with the clattering heels, her head tilted back to show dainty teeth as she laughed, the tip of her tongue inviting in the cave of her mouth, her thighs rubbing together to a hotel room where she would slap the bare buttocks of Antony Lord in protest and giggle before submitting to the thrust of his cock. And where was Norman? In recollection she was feverish. Yet in the long grass she had felt little – only the pallid whiteness of her thighs and his deftness. Afterwards there was a dull soreness. She listened to him grunting and felt nothing. Perhaps it was nerves. He smelled of suntan lotion. Next time it would be different. Anyway it was better than after the school dance in the bin shed with the meaty smell of school dinners rising out of the bins and the coldness of bare buttocks on the concrete. In the dance she was holding hands with her best friend. And Mr Burke the history teacher was watching her. He played the saxophone. Then she went outside with John Butler. He was wearing a maroon velvet jacket. He showed her the single Durex hidden in his inside pocket. 'Come prepared,' he said. Afterwards he slipped it off, tied a knot in it, and threw it into one of the bins. 'Pigs' swill,' he said. 'They feed those slops to the pigs. They eat my spunk. They eat my spunk and we eat them.'

Isobel yawned languorously, heaved herself to the edge of the bed and slid out on to the floor. This was easier than getting up. Falling was easier than rising. Anyway she was no longer in the bed. The floor was dusty. She crawled to the window and looked out.

Seeing Norman's empty sun-lounger below by the drooping geraniums in his front garden she realised that she had been hoping to see him out there oiling his tanned limbs and basking bare-chested and golden in the sunshine. The front windows of his house were closed – it looked as though the house were empty. Norman was probably out there in the railwayland sliding his brown fingers into the slippery vagina of some other girl. His mother was probably at bingo – trying to win a stupid prize. Fiona and Norman! Let me introduce you to my daughter-in-law. Her name is Fiona. Yes her father is a very educated man. Silly old bag.

Isobel felt sick when she saw Norman appear in the distance alone as if longing had conjured him up. And there was his mother following on behind, summery in a lavender-coloured dress and jacket. She stopped abruptly.

'Norman, Norman,' she called.

Her son turned and hurried towards her.

'Yes, mother,' he said.

'I need a few things from the shop. Will you come with me?'

Isobel saw Norman offer his mother his arm. It was as

if Sylvia were making time for her to wash, dress, brush her hair and run down the stairs so that, as Norman and Sylvia emerged from the shop together, Isobel was waiting for them, with a pair of secateurs, in the act of trimming the overgrown branches of the hedge that divided the dirty front garden of the blue house from the street.

'Hello,' she called out as they passed on the other side of the road.

'Hello, dear,' said Sylvia.

Norman looked at her, and as he turned away she saw that he was smiling. 'Nice day for a spot of gardening,' he said.

'Isn't it?' she replied, holding the secateurs ineptly in one hand and concentrating her gaze on their blunt and rusty blades. And when she raised her eyes, Sylvia and Norman were gone.

To stop the clumsy hedge trimming abruptly would be to demonstrate finally to those people, in the event of them watching her through the net curtains hanging so freshly in their windows, that the gardening was only a pretext. In fact the gardening was not just a pretext; the hedge was in urgent need of a trim. It was imperative that she continue in case they were watching. The blunt blades mashed the juicy stringing stems without severing the unwanted shoots; the shoots dangled messily from their branches. It was useless. Isobel fled into the house and slammed the door behind her.

She drank a cup of weak tea in the kitchen, fried herself a couple of eggs, and ate at the table with one leg crossed over the other, her head in her hand. They say that university is an exciting experience; she would meet many interesting people there.

Singing could be heard in the street. Isobel dipped a piece of bread into the yolk of her egg and chewed. 'Tie a Yellow Ribbon Round the Old Oak Tree'. It sounded like Norman. Where was he going? Isobel heard herself chewing inside her head. The pulp of bread and egg adhered to the roof of her mouth. Listening out for the stupid song she heard nothing and swallowed. Where was he going? There was no bread left in the bread bin. It would be a good idea to go out and get some in case her father returned. And yet if she did she might meet that idiot. She might meet that mummy's boy.

As she entered the corner shop who should she see by the bread stand but Norman, holding a basket that contained two packets of fancy biscuits and a tin of hot-dog sausages.

'Hello, Isobel,' he said, as she approached him casually down the aisle.

'Hello,' she answered.

'What are you looking for?' he asked, grinning at her and showing pink gums.

'Bread.'

'The staff of life,' said Norman, and laughed.

'Yes,' she said weakly.

He extended his hand and stroked her back. 'What are you looking for?' he asked her again. 'Who are you looking for?' he whispered.

'I am looking for a loaf of bread for my father.'

'Your father has gone away.'

'He might well return tonight. It being Sunday. How do you know anyway?'

'I know,' said Norman. 'You must be lonely all alone in that house.'

'I'm all right,' said Isobel.

She lifted a dry loaf off the rack and carried it to the till.

'Hello, hello, hello,' said the shopkeeper.

Isobel smiled at him. She paid for the bread and he wrapped it slowly. Norman was invisible behind a stack of cereal boxes. She made conversation with the shopkeeper to delay her departure so that there would be more time for Norman to act.

'Goodbye my sweetheart,' said the shopkeeper.

Isobel had to leave. Stepping out into the street it became clear that Norman was not following her.

Chips of mica glittered in the concrete of the pavement. It was broken and badly patched on the corner where shoppers parked their cars while they dashed into the shop and there were no children loitering by the fruit and vegetable display. The street was empty.

Isobel walked slowly in the sunshine. Norman was a fool. Even so he might have walked with her. Perhaps he would shout for her in a minute and run after her with his shopping in a carrier-bag. Hot-dog sausages. Maybe they were expecting guests. Maybe she should have waited for him. Isobel hoped that it was her who had been the rude one, the offhand hurtful cruel one. It was bearable if she had left him in the shop to wonder how she felt about him, and to feel his own ridiculousness. A black hollow dizziness projected Isobel furiously towards the empty house where she would cry painfully on her bed because Norman did not love her. She was crying already. Norman was a pig. It could be hoped that Norman did love her but was just testing her. Or that he was playing clever-clever, playing hard to get. But Isobel felt it – the knowing vain presumptuous pleasant lustful loveless charming indifference. That was it. And now she had got to the bottom of it her legs became weak. The concrete hurt the soles of her feet. A patchy world appeared to her through wet eyes and wet lashes. The world was empty. Her breath seared in scorching shallow gulps and she was empty. Crashing through the gate that swung on an oiled hinge between the untrimmed hedges she banged her knee. Once the front-door key was in the lock she turned it with her eyes closed and swallowed tears. Then the front door opened on to a hall thát smelled of fresh pipe smoke. Her father had returned.

Nine

'Hello Dad,' said Isobel, pushing open the door of the sitting room.

Antony Lord was reclining in an armchair as though he had been there for several hours; his head was thrown back, his thick hair parted on one side like a poet, and he rested his small feet on the edge of the fireguard. He was wearing brown pigskin boots and the bowl of his pipe fitted nicely into the palm of his hand. He stuck the chewed stem into his mouth, it was caught by the clenching of his little teeth, and he smiled. 'What have you been up to, my dear?' he asked, exhaling smoke from his nostrils.

'Where have you been?' Isobel replied.

'Do not worry,' said her father. 'Things will be better once you start college. Then you will make friends.'

'I hope so,' said Isobel. 'Would you like a sandwich?'

'No thank you, I have already eaten.'

'Oh.'

'What have you been doing with yourself in my absence?'

'Nothing much.'

'Aah. Nothing will come of nothing,' he said. 'Loneliness,' he added, pressing the tips of his fingers together.

'Have you been crying?'

'A bit,' she said.

'Aah. Never mind. You will make friends.'

Isobel sat down opposite her father in an armchair that matched his. 'Where have you been?' she asked.

'Never you mind.'

Isobel got up and walked out of the room. Antony was calling her name quite gently but she ignored him.

In the kitchen the blueness of fluorescent tubing dissolved the daylight and flickered, dispersing yellow shadows. Isobel made herself a sandwich of mayonnaise and tomatoes and carried it upstairs to her room. The bread was tough, she took a large bite and swallowed dryly; a seed stuck to her chin. And down below her father sucked the stem of his pipe in his red mouth.

On the windowsill the binoculars trailed a twisted leather strap in the dust. The binoculars were cold and heavy. Focusing on Norman's garden with her breasts pressed against the window frame the blur sharpened and yet there was nothing to see. There was nothing to see but the wilted geraniums, the empty sun-lounger and the billowing net curtains blinding in the sunshine.

Ten

The engorged womb bleats pain of spongy blood thickened to make a bed for an egg to be disgorged monthly unmet and yet it is the forty-seventh day and still the blood endures. Inside, a waggling finger meets the eye of the womb and waggles to encourage blood flow. Withdrawn, the finger is inspected; there is wrinkling and some shiny mucus but no blood.

My chin festers with pimples. The skin is raw and broken.

To induce abortion, a coat-hanger, presumably unbent, preferably sterilised, is stuck up the vagina and poked into the eye of the womb. Waggling waggling waggling the spongy lining is dislodged. And the foetus is dragged out as the coat-hanger is withdrawn. Or it slips out afterwards. Often it is unidentifiable. If you catch it early enough. It is like a clot of blood in appearance or a clot of slime or mucus. Red slime or red mucus. It is obviously best not to inspect the mess too closely. The whole operation could be described as the inducement of a heavy period. Although a nurse working at University College Hospital is reported to have said that she heard a foetus cry out as it was discarded.

Apparently the cry was like the mew of a cat. But that is not necessarily true. And there is another method. A bottle of gin and a hot bath. Then you have to throw yourself down the stairs. Or is that for suicide? Isobel smiled grimly. Poor little sod inside her as Norman would probably say. If she told him. Poor little sod.

The desire to vomit was nagging and yet the weighty inertia of her bloated body dragged against her effort to raise herself from the bed. The vomiting was making her gums sore. Up it came into her mouth and she had to stumble to the bathroom. The running tap was intended to disguise the sound of retching. Her throat was sore. She shut her eyes to avoid the sight of the vomit, it entered her nasal passages, and she was sick again.

Empty, one eye incarnadine, a blood vessel burst, her head lolling, hair lankly dangling over the lavatory bowl, the cartilage between her ribs bruised with the heave of vomiting, her soft sides aching, she rose ravenously from her knees and pulled the chain. Stiffly, hands cupping the weight of her breasts, she pigeon-stepped back to the bed beneath which she had stowed away her supplies.

The food she had chosen contained little nourishment; her craving was for the abrasively sour, salt or sweet. She ate lemon-curd out of the jar, scooping up the yellow jelly with her fingers, sucking it out of her fingernails and savouring the blistering sweetness, and several gherkins, fishing out the seeded dill to chew and drinking off the pickling liquid. Then twiglets and fishpaste. And again she was sick.

On her back the swelling of her belly was unnoticeable; it sank between her hipbones and disappeared. To lie on her back was therefore better than standing or curling on her side with her belly in her hands; on her back she could see that her belly was flat. Still her breasts were changed; a tender lumpy fullness grew inside them; the nipples were puckered; the whiteness was blue-veined.

It was a rank sickness now that plucked at her emptiness. It was not worth stumbling to the bathroom. Eyes closed she retched in the bed and spat out bile on to a corner of the sheet.

To fall, by accident, heroically out of a first or second floor window, breaking bones; to be transported in an ambulance, pale and broken under a red blanket, into the urgent hush of the hospital, close to death yet stoic, unafraid; to receive visits from a humbled father, unwashed and vigilant, a father casting mournful glances at the thin white patient; to see him perch on the bed gingerly, minding her mending limbs, and bravely smile; to raise one wasted hand; to forgive – how pleasant. What a dream to fill the emptiness.

There was no longer emptiness. Inside her a real pain was growing. The foetus. A baby. Its cries would wake her father. The blood-slimed and wriggling little creature could be held up and shoved in his face, smelling of the womb. He would hate it and she would love it.

Or he would smile at it and love it. A grandchild. How lovely. The umbilical cord uncut and connected, he would see the child and see her. With her legs open. Taking the child, he would take her. Loving the child, he would love her. And when the cord was severed, the love would endure.

And as for Norman the father, the unwitting, muscled, suntanned, mother's boy father, he would be proud of himself. Would he be proud? And what would Sylvia say? A girl or a boy. A grandchild. How nice!

Eleven

It was a dull dying summer morning, the rain falling softly on to dirty tarmac, the road and pavements warm. Isobel poked and prodded the secret growing inside her and held it close. The power warmed her; her father's mouth would fall open; the moment, however, was to be saved.

Unknowing, his plump hand would brush against her as they passed on the stairs. Unknowing he would touch her.

Unknowing, he would shout at her as usual, scream at her, raging, or turn a silent, clever, hirsute cheek in his ignorance, unable to touch her.

And then she would tell him. That would give him something to scream about. But the moment was to be saved. She would hold the secret close and enjoy it until she was ready. The power was delightful. She would move him.

In her nightgown she entered the kitchen and there he was dismembering a chicken in his pyjamas. His hands were fatty.

'Hello, Dad,' she said cheerfully.

Antony raised his head and looked at her. 'So cheerful?' he asked. 'You look awful.'

'Thank you darling,' said Isobel. 'I'll put the kettle on.'

'Don't bother. There's tea in the pot,' he said.

'Well, well, well,' said Isobel.

'And what the hell is that supposed to mean?'

'What, dear?'

'Oh shut up.'

'Yes, dear father,' said Isobel, smiling sweetly.

The chicken flesh was pallid and sinewed beneath the pimply skin. The bones splintered as they were broken. Inside the pearly broken leg joint the marrow was clotted red. Small pieces of skin and gristle clung to Antony's hands.

'Oh my God,' said Isobel, and vomited into the kitchen sink.

'Turn the tap on,' said Antony. 'Are you all right?'

Isobel retched and vomited and washed out her mouth. A slimy strand of hair was stuck to her face. 'Fine,' she said.

Antony looked at her closely. 'You look green,' he said.

'I'll go and have a wash then.'

Isobel returned from the bathroom, her face blotched and shining in scraped patches where scrubbing had removed the dead cell surface of her skin. She sat down at the table and turned her face away from the fishy smell of thawed chicken. A mess of blood and water was seeping out of the heap of flesh.

'What are you making?' she asked.

'Curry,' said Antony.

Isobel heaved.

He began to slice the chicken into bite-sized pieces, paring the pale flesh from the bones.

'I thought we could have lunch together. I thought it might cheer you up.'

'Dad,' said Isobel.

'What?'

'I'm pregnant.'

Her father received the news calmly. 'I see. And who is the father of this . . . er child?'

'Norman. You know. From over the road.'

'Oh Norman. I see. I assume you intend to terminate this pregnancy?'

'No.'

'I see. I gather that you intend to have the baby.'

'Yes.'

'Aah,' he said. 'Is this wise? You are hardly more than a child yourself. Have you thought clearly about this? A child needs a father, you know.'

'You can be its father,' said Isobel.

'Hardly,' said Antony Lord.

The secret was out. He was unmoved.

Norman, handsome in morning dress, stepping out smartly, a carnation fixed to his lapel with a safety-pin, a shaft of stained sunlight illuminating his golden head (does the groom kneel at the altar or merely bow his head amongst the flowers, lilies and white lilac, the fragrance in the dusty church), says I do, not I will, and lifts the veil to kiss the bride. The vicar offers stern words of advice. And who is the best man? How far gone are you? A lump is visible inside the bridal gown, swelling the fall of heavy silk and lace. I'd get rid of it if I were you. Hands clasp bearing bands of gold. Norman would love to wear a ring. And the bride collapses, losing blood that splashes on to the altar cloth, and dies in childbirth. The baby is dead. Or if not, there would be a quiet reception. Mrs Sylvia Brake and Mr Antony Lord request the pleasure of your company.

Isobel, having regained her slim figure, in a dress of blue cotton with a white collar and stiff cuffs, pushes a pram along the high street and stops for a moment to bend over the baby and gurgle. Powdered milk is given at bedtime to fortify the diet of mother's milk; it gives mother more independence and helps baby sleep. Here comes Norman in his uniform. He looks handsome in his postman's cap.

'Norman,' said Isobel. 'I'm pregnant.'

'How far gone are you?'

'I'm having it,' she said.

'Why?'

'I want to have a baby.'

'Why?'

Isobel raised her pleading eyes to him. 'I don't know,' she said.

'I see.'

'That's exactly what my father said.'

'Great minds think alike,' said Norman, and smiled, his lips parting decorously to reveal his perfect teeth.

Isobel began to cry.

'Don't cry,' said Norman.

She turned her white and shaking face towards him. 'You are going to be a father,' she said.

'I had gathered that.'

'Well?'

'Can't you get rid of it? I don't think it's a very good idea.'

'Why not?'

'You haven't got a clue. What about your famous last words and all that? "I look death in the face" and all that? What will you say on your deathbed? "I had a baby." Big deal. What about your plans?'

'Norman, I want to have a baby.'

'All right, all right, have a baby,' he said.

'Thank you, I will,' said Isobel.

They sat in silence side by side on the sofa.

'I feel sick,' said Isobel.

'So do I,' said Norman.

Isobel stood up. 'I'm going,' she said.

'I'll go and tell mother,' he said.

Twelve

'Mother,' he shouted.

The empty kitchen was neat and clean. Three freshly boiled dishcloths were folded and drying on the back of a chair. In the sink a mug half-full of tea stood waiting to be washed up, dried and hung on its hook.

'Mother,' Norman shouted into the dark mouth of the staircase. There was no answer. He mounted the stairs. 'Mother,' he said.

The bathroom door was open. The bath was scoured and dry. A razor and a tube of shaving cream had been placed on the side of the basin next to a jar holding two toothbrushes and a tube of toothpaste. A bar of pink soap lay in its dish. On the window ledge there was a bottle of sun-tan oil and a flowered cardboard drum containing talcum powder. The bath mat hung as usual over the side of the bath.

Her bedroom door was closed. Norman opened it and breathed the sweet stale odour of powder emanating from her bed and her wardrobe. Her hairbrush lay on the seat of a chair; among the pale bristles a few hairs were twisted. The bed was lumpy and sagging under its candlewick bedspread. It looked so soft and comfortable Norman lowered himself on to it, removed his shoes, and closed his eyes.

Sylvia's dry brown hand slipped in between the arm and side of Mr Green, scratched by the rough tweed of his new jacket. She had to adjust her long stride so that it would fit in with Mr Green's short step. He was wearing soft suede shoes. It was Sunday. His little dog scampered along behind.

Crossing the road by the corner shop they walked in silent anticipation of the silence after parting and parted on the pavement outside Sylvia's house.

'Goodbye,' Mr Green shouted.

Sylvia opened the door and closed it softly behind her. Norman came leaping down the stairs.

'Who was that old sod?' he asked.

'That old sod was Mr Green.'

'I see.'

'Oh do you,' said Sylvia inaudibly.

'Mother, I have something to tell you,' said Norman.

'Not now dear.'

'Please mother. Please.'

'Oh Norman. I'm tired. Exhausted. What is it?'

'Come up the pub with me. It's easier to talk there.'

'If I must dear. When it opens.'

The George was crowded with familiar faces. Sylvia chose a table by the snack counter where they might not be overheard.

'I'll get them in,' said Norman, at the bar. 'What will you have?'

'A lager shandy for me, Norman. Make it a half please dear.'

'Right you are. A lager shandy for mother and a pint of lager for me. And have one for yourself,' said Norman.

'Thanks, I don't mind if I do,' said the barmaid. 'You're nice. I'm new,' she added.

'Oh,' said Norman. 'Are you?'

64

The barmaid looked at him. 'Well, quite new. Newish,' she said.

'Right,' he said, looking away.

Sylvia was comfortably settled, stretching her legs out and rotating her feet slowly under the table; Norman could see the soles of her shoes.

'With someone?' said the barmaid.

'Yes I am. My mother,' said Norman.

The barmaid laughed. 'What's your problem?' she asked.

Norman turned suddenly as if in anger and stared. 'As a matter of fact I am involved, at this very moment, in a serious family crisis,' he muttered.

'Ooo get you,' said the barmaid, and held out her hand. 'One pound and ninety-five pence. Please. That's with half a lager for me.'

Norman paid and carried the drinks one in each hand over to his mother.

'Well?' said Sylvia. 'Spit it out.'

Norman took a small sip of beer and swallowed. 'Isobel is pregnant,' he said.

'Oh dear,' said Sylvia. 'What a silly-billy.'

'I know,' said Norman.

'Who is she going with?'

'What do you mean? No one,' said Norman.

'You!' said Sylvia, her closed face opening into a triumphant smile. 'You'll have to marry her, Norman. It's about time you settled down. You will marry her won't you dear?'

'Marry her, mother?'

'Yes dear. For me. You would make me truly happy. I have not been truly happy since your father went away.'

'Yes, mother,' said Norman. 'I will.'

'Good. That's settled then,' said Sylvia.

'Oh look. There's Mr Green,' said Norman.

'Oh yes. So it is,' said Sylvia.

Mr Green waved cordially and took his place in the snug with Mr Elbrooke and Mr Mackenzie.

'Silly sod,' said Norman. 'Drink up. I want to go home.'

Thirteen

'Father, I've told Norman,' said Isobel.

'Aah,' said Antony Lord. 'Well done.'

The insidious smell of curry seeped out of the carpet and curtains and sickened Isobel.

'Can I open a window?'

'Go ahead,' said her father, sinking deeper into his armchair. 'You missed lunch,' he said. 'Delicious.'

'Oh,' said Isobel.

'And what did young Norman have to say for himself?'

Isobel adjusted her position on the sofa. 'He said "all right have a baby".'

'Is that all?'

'No. He said "I'll go and tell mother".'

'Ah,' said Antony. 'What is he going to do about it?'

'I don't know.'

'How do you feel about him?'

'I don't know.'

'You don't know,' said Antony.

Isobel made a small noise. Her throat was taut. 'He's a mother's boy,' she said.

'Why do you want him then?'

'I don't know. Do I want him?'

'I don't know.'

There was a knock at the front door.

'I'll go,' said Antony, striding with relief out of the room. Isobel heard him whistling casually in the hall. Antony opened the front door.

'Good evening,' said Norman.

'Come in, come in,' said Antony, luring Norman into the hall with embracing arms and stripping him of his jacket. Then he began to pat the guest on the back, batting and shooing him into the sitting-room.

Isobel rose to receive him, bestowing on him a weak smile and inclining towards him involuntarily.

'Hello,' she said.

Norman smiled at Antony, who was standing in the doorway as if to prevent escape, and said 'Would you leave us?'

'By all means,' said Antony. 'I'll be in my study,' he added, and left.

'Isobel, will you marry me?' said Norman.

Isobel sat down heavily. 'What?'

'I said will you marry me.'

'No,' said Isobel. 'No. Thank you all the same. I won't.'

'Why not?'

'I don't want to.'

'Ah,' said Norman.

Isobel was unable to stop herself from grinning with pleasure. 'Thank you so much. For asking. It's just that I want to stay here with my dad. At home.'

'I'll be going then,' said Norman.

Isobel held out her hand to him. Norman took it and converted the gesture into a formal handshake. 'Goodbye,' he said.

After the front door had closed behind him Isobel ran upstairs to her father. She opened the study door and found him making notes in a red notebook. 'Guess what?' she shouted.

Antony dropped his pen. 'What?'

He asked me to marry him.'

'He didn't!'

'He did!'

'And?'

'I refused him.'

'Aah,' said Antony. 'I see. You refused him. Well I suppose we'll manage,' he said.

Isobel began to move towards her father.

'No don't start that,' he said. 'Clear off. Go away and leave me in peace.'

'Thanks Dad,' said Isobel. 'We'll manage.'

Norman stood on the doorstep of the blue house and struggled to get into his jacket.

'Phew,' he said.

He could return to his mother now. Isobel wanted to remain at home with her father. Fair enough. There was little point anyway in her marrying. Still a dull agitation or unease made the short walk home a slow one for Norman; his relief was undercut by a bad feeling he was unable to name.

Sylvia was waiting for him in the front room. 'Mission accomplished?'

'She refused me,' said Norman.

'Nonsense. That girl is pregnant. She must want to marry.'

'She doesn't, mother.'

'In that case she isn't pregnant. Fiona is not pregnant. That's rumbled her then the little prat.'

'She is not called Fiona. You don't know her. She wants to stay at home with her father.'

Sylvia heaved herself on to her feet and stood swaying with her legs apart. 'You didn't ask her!'

'I did. She refused me. There is no point in her marrying and moving a few doors down the road.'

'What?' Sylvia roared.

'Uh Uh' said Norman, his jaw hanging slackly and his eyes black with panic.

'What the fuck makes you think I want her here?'

'I thought we could all live together. I want to stay at home with you. Anyway, she refused me.'

'Oh so that's all right then is it?'

'What do you mean?'

'Norman stays at home with mummy. Little icky bitty Norman stays at home with mumsie wumsie eh?'

'This is my home.'

'For fuck's sake, Norman.'

Sylvia's great bellow dropped away when she saw Norman's face. 'Oh Norman,' she said. 'I'm sorry. Never mind.'

There was silence between them and then Norman spoke.

'Why did she refuse me? There is a part of me in her.'

'She refused you because she wants to stay at home with her father.'

'Why did you tell me to ask her?'

'I did not think that anyone could refuse you anything.'

'Why did you want me to marry?'

'Because I think it's time you made a home for yourself. I won't last for ever you know.'

'Don't,' said Norman. 'Don't say that.'

'She might come round,' said Sylvia.

'She won't. I'm glad she refused me. I don't want her. I want to stay here with you.'

'Oh Norman,' said Sylvia, and sat down beside him. She could say no more.

Fourteen

Autumn glowered, dead yellow, sodden brown, and the sky was brackish. Outside the low building there was a ramp for pushchairs, wheelchairs and prams. The fence edging the ramp and the doors of the building were painted cheerful colours, to welcome you to the Health Centre – sunshine yellow and red. The approach was planted with sturdy evergreens through which the path from the street curved, making the short journey longer. Pregnant women made their way through the bushes towards the building to receive their ante-natal care. Escorted by mothers and sisters, arms linked in support, or alone, efficient or bewildered, hands placed in the small of the back or pushing prams full of children, followed by more children, the women heaved and panted up the ramp and pushed open the door. Isobel was among them, wearing sensible shoes, her hair tied back with a ribbon, a warm overcoat buttoned up across her chest.

In the waiting-room, their feet up, and in the lavatories, where they lingered, the women asked each other questions. 'How far gone are you?' 'What about your old man?' 'What did sister say about your legs?'

Isobel leant on the counter at reception and peered through the hatch.

'I'd like to see Dr Grant, please. I'm pregnant,' she said, loudly.

'Have you brought a sample, dear?' asked the receptionist.

'Yes.'

'Please take a seat.'

'Thank you very much.'

The chairs in the waiting-room were upholstered in hairy orange tweed. Isobel picked up a magazine and sat down. A lissome well-scrubbed face smiled up at her out of the centre pages. An old man lowered himself into the seat next to her, his red eyes gummed-up.

'Waiting long?' he asked.

'Yes,' said Isobel.

'It's the cuts,' the man said. 'They lay off the doctors. The patients die. Less mouths for them to feed,' he said.

'Yes,' said Isobel. 'Terrible.'

The receptionist called from her cubicle. 'Isobel Lord.'

The surgery was small and odourless.

'Hello,' said Dr Grant. 'Come in. Come in. Please sit down. How are you my dear?' He looked at his notes. 'Isobel. How are you?'

'I'm pregnant.'

'Ah, I see.'

'That's what they all say,' said Isobel.

'What?'

'Nothing.'

'Do you have a sample? A urine sample?'

'Yes.'

'The first one of the day?'

'Yes.'

'Good girl. Leave it at reception on your way out. I'm afraid it will be a week at least until I can give you the result. There is a backlog at the lab. Understaffed,' he said.

'Never mind. I know I'm pregnant,' said Isobel.

'Ah, I see. How do you feel?'

'I feel fine.'

'Good. Good. I assume that you want to have this child?'

'Yes.'

'Good,' said the doctor. 'Come in and see me in a week or so. When I have the result of your test I can book you into the ante-natal clinic at the hospital and they will help you organise everything. And there are, as you know, ante-natal classes at this health centre which I can recommend highly. Exercise, relaxation, and such. Birth can be such a pleasurable experience if you are properly prepared. I can see from your notes that you are unmarried. Who is the father of your child?'

'I am a single parent,' said Isobel. 'He asked me to marry him but I don't want to. I am going to live at home with my father.'

'Good. Fine. You seem to be a very sensible young lady.'

'Thank you,' said Isobel.

'Congratulations,' said the doctor. 'Bringing a new life into the world is a marvellous thing. Goodbye, my dear.'

The brown street was lined with trees; leaves were falling or fallen. Isobel touched the trunks with cold fingers as she passed. The world is full of pregnant women. I will love my baby and my baby will love me. The world is full of babies. One pram, one cot, one baby bath. Nappies, bottles, a steriliser. Zinc and castor oil cream B.P. Baby powder, baby lotion, baby oil. Vests, pants, gloves, hats, booties, babygrows and tights. A shawl, cardigans, small dresses, nightgowns, socks. Sheets and blankets, towels, cotton buds, cotton wool and baby soap. As soft as skin, a piece of creamy wool is stitched by hand and gathered into a tiny yoke to make a tiny coat. The border is embroidered; as red as blood, the petals of poppies shaded from scarlet to white; as blue as sky, the black-eyed cornflower, its grey leaves slender and fading to silver; and yellow as butter the daisies. To unwrap, out of folds of tissue paper, a gown of white muslin, pin-tucked and gathered and starched. To unfurl the skirt, a trellis of branches stitched and appliquéd, budded with french knots and blooming, white on white. The hem is rolled and scalloped with innumerable tiny stitches, white as milk. The baby will be a girl. It will be a girl like me. Here comes a woman pushing a pram as she advances under the trees. The bulk of the woman is tented in a dark and shapeless garment. Her legs stick out from underneath as solid as a side of beef. In her fat face her mouth is pinched. A pair of plastic carrier bags, misshapen with shopping, hang from the handle of the pram. The baby is slender and perfect, wrapped in a tartan blanket. Its eyes are open. It is looking up through trees at the sky.

Naked, a chair jammed under the door handle to prevent intrusion, the light bulb shedding a smeary, private light into the daytime gloom of curtains closed against the world, Isobel gently stroked her distended body. The abdomen showed veins through stretched skin and her legs looked absurdly thin with the little pot slung between her hipbones above them. Her father might pat it affectionately or laugh at her hugeness or sigh at the cost. Norman might shy away in terror or lust after it and her. The doctor would examine it and measure it with his instruments. Men would whistle at her. They could see that she had been fucked at least once. They would imagine her doing it, but they could not imagine her own private pleasure. Walking out with a lump under a smock afforded a certain delight; people love a pregnant woman. They might smile and nod and whistle and shout and give pleasure but they could not share the exultation.

Fifteen

It is not clear whether they are doing it or not; the man, dressed in new and voluminous tweeds, has got the woman up against a wall and it looks like he is grinding away at the right place, but it is unlikely – he is by no means young, and having it away in a public place, even at night, is usually frowned upon by respectable gents, however dapper. You never know though, given half a chance.

One of the woman's knees is just visible, poking out from behind the man's overcoat; it looks as though it is shaking. The flesh looks loose – she must be old too. The railwayland is usually deserted at night.

Is it possible to fuck standing up? They do it in the films. It must depend on the respective heights of the man and the woman. If the woman is small, the man can lift her off the ground and she can sit on his dick with her legs gripped around his waist. That would help take the weight off his arms. If the woman is large, it might be easier; she could stand with her legs open and the man could approach her from below. It was hard to tell the height of this woman because her head was bowed and hidden.

Norman watched from the cover of the derelict shed

74

and saw her big soft feet planted firmly on the ground. A small dog was playing nearby in the long grass.

There was much movement inside the man's overcoat. The woman's hand appeared at the back of his neck, large and freckled. Norman saw that it was his mother's hand. The man was Mr Green. They were shaking together inside his overcoat. 'Oooh, ooh,' she cried as she came.

It was his mother's voice. Mr Green was fumbling with his flies.

'Sylvia,' he said. 'Sylvia.'

Then he passed her a handkerchief. That was to wipe his spunk out of her cunt.

Norman crouched behind the broken shed and cried like a child. He made a shuddering silence between sobs; the gaps in his lament were filled for him by the lovers' fumble and pant; he listened and his mother laughed as she picked her way through brambles and rubble; he cried until they were gone.

Emerging out of shelter into a miserable wind he staggered across the dismal railwayland under a yellow sky. His mother's footsteps were messy in the patch of sterile mud where nothing grew. His feet fell where her feet had fallen. He began to run.

Before knocking on the door of the blue house he wiped his running nose on his cuff. This time his mother had not sent him. The door opened.

'Hello,' said Isobel. 'Are you all right?'

'No,' said Norman. 'Can I come in?'

'Of course. Please do. He is out.'

'Good,' said Norman. 'I have had a bad experience.'

'Oh dear,' said Isobel. 'You are in a state. Come and sit down by the fire. Would you like a drink?'

'Yes,' said Norman.

Isobel poured him a large glass of whisky. 'Well?' she asked.

'I just watched mother getting fucked by Mr Green in the railwayland.'

'Oh my God. Are you sure?'

'I watched them. She had an orgasm. I heard her cooing and sighing.'

'Oh Norman,' said Isobel.

'I've never fucked anyone standing up,' he said.

'Have another drink,' said Isobel.

'Thank you, I will. I went for a nice quiet walk in the railwayland. I heard him whispering her name. Fucking whore,' he said.

'Who is this Mr Green?'

'Fuck knows,' said Norman. 'Some bloke.'

'I know how you feel,' said Isobel.

'I can't bear it,' said Norman, wailing.

'You've got to.'

Isobel took his hand.

Out of present coldness it was impossible to imagine the hot days of summer, the heat that had drawn Norman half-naked out of his house and laid him out, the sunshine that had dragged Isobel on her hands and knees to her window to spy; how she had pictured him paying her visits and how she had longed for him! And now here they were together like any husband and wife in front of the fire on a cold November evening. Except that Norman was crying for his mother.

'Never mind,' said Isobel, stroking his hair.

'I do mind,' said Norman, his head in her lap.

'She made me ask you,' he said. 'She made me propose to you.'

'I thought so,' said Isobel quietly. 'It cheered me up anyway.'

'You refused me.'

'I know.'

'I didn't want you,' said Norman.

'I know,' said Isobel. 'Why are you crying?'

'You didn't want me.'

Isobel smiled.

'I hadn't thought that you might not want me,' said

76

Norman. 'She sent me out blithely to ask you. I thought it was for your sake. A grandchild. How nice! You did not want me. I thought I was glad. You know, relieved. But when I got home I saw what her game was. She was angry that you did not want me because she wanted Mr Green. It was for his sake. She wanted Mr Green, not me.'

Norman became silent suddenly as if to concentrate better on this fact.

'Don't dwell on it,' said Isobel. 'Think about the baby.'

Norman removed the chewed knuckle from his mouth. 'Perhaps the baby will love me,' he said.

'I've got my first ante-natal appointment soon,' said Isobel.

'Do you want me to come with you?'

'No,' she replied. 'I'll go on my own.'

Sixteen

The hospital, a great streaked edifice castellated and turret-
ed under dripping roofs of blue slate, cast a grim half-light
over the extension buildings and galvanised waste-bins that
stood at the foot of its towering walls.

Isobel made a dignified journey from the main gates to
the maternity department, passing groups of lovely nurses
crowned in starched white caps. She saw the scarlet lining
of their cloaks as they hurried across the windy courtyard,
their legs brushing together under the fresh striped skirts
of their uniforms, and smiled at their motherly faces. Her
appointment was at one o'clock. It was nearly time. Above
a pair of double doors she saw a large red sign – 'Ante-
Natal Clinic'.

'We are running late,' said the receptionist. 'It may
be a long wait.'

Isobel went to the lavatory, taking her time over the
washing and drying of her hands. She rubbed her hands
together under the hot air machine until her skin became
silky. In the mirror she saw her own face beside the faces
of the other women. It was strange to see how fierce and
angry they were, or how tired and sad. But when they

looked at themselves, raising their eyes from the wash basins and the soap dispensers, their faces softened; they hitched up their mouths and almost smiled. Her own face was beautiful.

The coffee machine was broken. Isobel inserted her ten-pence piece and waited for a cup to fall. There was no cup. Granules of coffee scattered out of their chute on to the floor and then there was a shower of powdered milk. She cast about for a cup but there were none lying around to catch these excretions. Hot water trickled out and dribbled down the front of the machine, making a dirty puddle on the carpet.

The women were waiting in a large hall furnished with banks of upholstered benches, facing a small door behind which the examinations took place. At irregular intervals, the door opened to admit a new patient or allow a patient to leave. Sometimes there was a collision in the narrow doorway followed by laughter or shouting.

Isobel sat down and stared at the small door and waited. The waiting was interminable. The grey blankness of the door made her give up hope – it was closed as if never to re-open. Perhaps it was the wrong door. She looked to the right and left but there was no other. When it finally opened it almost made her gasp. A big fat woman came waddling out. Then it was closed again.

Staring at the door made her eyes water. And yet to look away was impossible; if she turned her eyes to inspect the mothers-to-be who waited placidly as if they had all the time in the world or paced anxiously in the aisle casting mournful glances at the large clock, the long hand of which jerked visibly from one minute to the next, the door might open and the nurse might pop out and call her name. Then she would miss her appointment. 'You will have to wait,' the nurse would say.

The woman who sat next to Isobel nudged her and spoke. 'I want to go to the toilet,' she said. 'If they call me out, will you tell them?'

'What time is your appointment?'

'Eleven-thirty. My name is Mrs Fernandez. Maria Fernandez.'

It was half past two.

'All right,' said Isobel. 'You'd better be quick though.'

'Thanks,' said the woman, and lumbered off towards the lavatories.

Just as she disappeared the door opened. The nurse stood there examining her clip-board. 'Mrs Fernandez,' she called.

Isobel hurried towards her.

'Hello Maria,' said the nurse. 'How are we today?'

'I am not Mrs Fernandez.'

'Well go and sit down then,' said the nurse.

'Mrs Fernandez is in the lavatory.'

'Too bad,' said the nurse, looking at the list of names. 'Mrs Godley,' she called.

'That's not fair,' said Isobel. 'Mrs Fernandez's appointment was at eleven-thirty. She has been waiting for three hours.'

'Too bad,' said the nurse, and ushered Mrs Godley in through the door.

Isobel returned to her seat. Mrs Fernandez reappeared after a couple of minutes.

'They called you,' said Isobel. 'You missed your turn. I'm sorry. I tried to explain but it didn't work.'

'Not your fault,' said Mrs Fernandez, and sat down.

They waited side by side in silence. And then suddenly Mrs Fernandez stood up and began to shout. She stood in the middle of the hall and bellowed, her hands fluttering in the air above her head. The waiting women clucked at her and tittered. 'You waste my fucking life,' she shouted. Her face was white. Isobel tried to calm her but Mrs Fernandez pushed her away. 'My fucking life is wasting here,' she shouted. Then she sunk spent on to the bench and wept into a little lace-edged handkerchief.

The door opened.

'Mrs Fernandez,' the nurse called.

Mrs Fernandez, wet-faced and timid, crept towards the door.

At half-past four the Christmas tree in the corner of the hall by the coffee machine was illuminated; the fairy lights winked on and off, on and off, on and off. Isobel put her feet up on the bench and continued to wait. There were many empty seats now on the upholstered benches. A woman was sleeping, her head resting on her chest. Bored children sulked and cried. A small boy curled up in his mother's lap and went to sleep. A man arrived, bringing chips to feed his waiting family. Isobel smelled the vinegar hungrily. The easy breathing of the sleeping woman could be heard in the waiting stillness.

There was time to think as the clock ticked. There was nothing to do now but wait. Perhaps that was how Norman spent his time. He had all the time in the world – time for spying on his mother, time to cry. Antony did not have the time for such things. He never cried. Now she was pregnant it was as if she too had all the time in the world. And this was doing something anyway, waiting for the baby. You had to rest and look after yourself. She did not feel like crying. It was as if time had stopped. When the baby arrived it would begin again. Then she would see. It would be clearer. Until then she waited.

The door opened.

'Isobel Lord,' the nurse called.

The greeting offered to Isobel was peremptory; the nurses and doctors were tired and fed up; the foetus was no more to them by the end of the day than any other growth to be monitored, tested and measured. The foetus was probably a healthy little creature with two arms and two legs. Or maybe it had one leg and two arms. One arm and two legs. Three legs. No head. Two heads. No brain. Three eyes. Muscular dystrophy. Down's syndrome. A hole in the heart. A penis and a vagina. Scales. Fur. Or it might be dead. It might have died of grief and rotted inside her. The swelling of her abdomen could have been caused by gas expelled from a decaying foetus. It could be twins. Or triplets. A dwarf or a giant. A freak. Its small horned head would appear on the screen, it would hide its hairy face in shame behind its scaly hands and peep out with pleading eyes between its fingers. Isobel managed to retain the appearance of calm; she smiled patiently and co-operated; and yet in her womb a monstrous black panic was rearing against her. The monster was gnawing away at the spongy lining and eating her up. Having waited three and three-quarter hours for her appointment, Isobel found the lack of dazzling scientific equipment disappointing; she said so to the nurse, hoping to appear normal – she was expecting a bank of screens and panels and dials. Instead the doctor told her to fill in a pile of forms, and recorded her weight and blood pressure in a little book. Then there was a physical examination, a blood test and more questions. She was asked to drink a large quantity of water and wait around until it entered the bladder. This was prior to the scan. Isobel thought she would burst or piss herself on the trolley. They smeared her abdomen with cool jelly and passed the scanner back and forth. A greyish picture of the baby came up on the screen. It was difficult to read the picture. The doctor pointed out the head and limbs.

'Don't tell me whether it is a boy or a girl,' said Isobel. She could not tell. The picture was vague and blurred. 'What do you think?' she asked. 'Is it all right?'

'Perfect. Good girl,' said the doctor.

Isobel looked at her baby on the screen. 'It's beautiful,' she said. 'I knew it would be.'

Seventeen

The table was laid with an odd assortment of crockery. Several large fine white plates, crested and gold-rimmed, looked like the remains of a dissipated inheritance or a bargain from a junk shop; two solid earthenware dishes, a souvenir of Provençal holidays, dragged up memories of charcuterie, olives and boeuf en daube; two ancient willow patterns and six ivy-bordered Wedgwood Napoleons were stacked up under a pile of knives and forks, beside an enamel water jug and a pile of paper napkins. The paper napkins were bright green.

'Sit down, sit down,' said Morris, the host.

Four or five young women were already seated at the table. There were no introductions. Isobel and Antony took their places. Morris opened another bottle of wine and sent one of the girls for more glasses. Antony looked around him and spoke. 'I am unable, after all these years, and how many years is it, since we last met? It must be three or more – I am unable, as I said, to distinguish, clearly and with confidence, between one of your lovely daughters and another. That is, I presume that all these delightful . . . er creatures are your daughters. It is so simple for me, having but one . . . Are you the eldest? Or perhaps the youngest? It is, in fact, impossible to tell. And yet somehow I feel that you are Miranda, Miranda who was, at nine, so very clever at drawing. Do you still draw?'

'I am Jane,' said the girl.

'Aah! Of course. You, unlike your name, are not plain, sweet Jane, if I may say so.'

The girl smiled politely.

'I ramble on,' said Antony. 'Sweet Jane,' he said, and sighed.

Isobel heard her father's inanities with the indifference of the self-possessed; nothing he could say now would make her squirm. She sat there at the table chewing placidly on a slice of wholemeal bread and listened, quite without the desire to speak.

'I am Miranda,' said the girl who sat next to Isobel. 'I am the youngest,' she said, trying to rescue Antony from the embarrassment of his faulty memory. She was small and dark, with melancholy eyes. Jane was large and blonde. Antony felt no embarrassment; it was as if, under cover of his beard, his age and his manhood, he could say anything he liked to these lovely young creatures; with them he could do as he pleased. Morris had gone down into the basement to bring up more wine. His wife was in the kitchen. There was, therefore, no limit to the scope for stupidity, gallantry and ridiculousness.

'Of course,' said Antony. 'You are Miranda. It is clear to me now. You have the incisive eyes of the artist.'

This was too much. Miranda laughed. 'Not quite,' she said. 'Medicine. I am going to be a doctor.'

'Exquisite,' said Antony, undeterred. 'A woman of beauty and intelligence is a rare thing indeed.'

Miranda and Jane exchanged a sly glance of amusement and Isobel saw their mocking eyes. 'Father is a bit old-fashioned,' she said.

Morris entered the dining-room, his arms full of bottles.

'In fact, he hasn't got a clue,' said Isobel.

'My loyal daughter speaks,' said Antony, raising his glass. 'To Isobel!'

'It's his nerves. His shyness makes him stupid,' she said. 'Cheers.'

'Being a father is a hazardous occupation,' said Morris, and left the room. Everybody laughed.

The sound of banging reached them from the front door. More guests were arriving. Men's voices were raised in shouts of greeting and a woman laughed. Antony leapt to his feet as they entered the dining-room and embraced them one by one. The woman he held in his arms tenderly. He kissed her on the forehead and led her over to Isobel.

'This is my daughter,' he said. 'I think it is time that you met.'

'Hello,' said Isobel. There was an empty chair beside her. 'Why don't you sit down?'

'Thank you,' said the woman.

'My name is Valerie. I burst into your room once. Do you remember? I was looking for the lavatory. Your father said that you were ill in bed and didn't want to see anyone. How pale you looked then! I wanted to sit with you or make you some broth or something. You looked so poorly. But Antony said to leave well alone.'

'How kind,' said Isobel. 'I'm better now anyway. I'm pregnant,' she said, and laughed.

'How marvellous! Can I feel it?' said Valerie.

Isobel nodded. The woman pressed her hand gently on to Isobel's stomach. Gaining confidence, she began to stroke firmly. Then her hand moved from beneath Isobel's breasts to the top of her thighs.

'I have no children,' said the woman.

'It's never too late,' said Isobel, and coloured.

The woman was at least forty. Or even fifty. Her soft old face was hanging with sadness.

'It is,' said Valerie.

'I'm sorry.'

When Valerie smiled her face looked young. 'That's

85

the way it goes,' she said. 'Antony didn't tell me you were having a baby.'

'He's like that. Do you see him a lot?'

'Two or three times a week.'

'Since when?'

'Since that party. At your place. When you were ill.'

'I see,' said Isobel.

Morris's wife staggered into the room, carrying a huge dish; two legs of lamb, steaming fragrantly and seasoned with garlic, lay side by side in the middle, surrounded by several pounds of golden roast potatoes. The guests began to cheer.

'I'm starving,' said Isobel.

Valerie patted her on the thigh. Miranda followed her mother from the kitchen, carrying a bowl of buttered sprouts in one hand and a salad in the other.

'I'll carve,' said Antony.

The meal began.

The bowls of salad and vegetables were passed up and down the table; glasses were filled and emptied and filled again; their guests cleared their plates and held them out for more. There was much shouting, and laughter. A man fell off his chair. Morris's wife became scarlet in the face, lowered her eyes and protested modestly as the food was praised. Her husband clapped her on the back. Jane was shouting at Antony.

'What a racket,' said Valerie.

'Yes,' said Isobel, finishing her third helping of potatoes. 'I feel tired, carrying this weight around. And I can't stop eating.'

'You look well on it,' said Valerie.

'Thanks.'

Jane's voice was shrill. 'Fool!' she shouted. 'Coward!'

Antony stood up. 'I admit defeat,' he said, bowing gracefully to Jane, and edged his way calmly round the table. Standing behind Isobel's chair he raised his small pale hands and grinned, rubbing them together. 'Hello ladies. How are you my dears?' He laid his left hand on Valerie's shoulder. He laid his right hand on the back of Isobel's neck.

'Isobel is tired,' said Valerie.

'Shall we go?' Antony asked.

'I want my pudding first,' said Isobel.

The pudding was served. It was trifle. Antony ate his perched between Isobel and Valerie, his left buttock on one chair, his right buttock on the other. Then they went home.

The fire in the grate was dying; faint red embers and the black edges of unburnt coals were powdered with white ashes. Antony knelt, poker in hand, and stirred its remains. A fine dust rose in his face and he coughed. The stirring kindled flame. Lump by lump he piled new coal on to the stirred embers; his fingers were blackened; he left the room to wash his hands.

'How are you feeling?' Valerie asked.

'Fine,' said Isobel.

Valerie was the one who had reason to feel bad. Valerie was the old one, childless, wasted and finished. Valerie's voice was dense with concern and sincerity. 'I hope this is not a strain for you, Isobel. I mean me and Antony. I think he thought you might mind. Not that he said anything. You know what he is like.'

'I don't mind,' said Isobel. 'It's nice for him to have a friend.'

Valerie looked motherly; her bosom was enormous and her bovine eyes mild. Any minute now she will call me darling. She will not be able to contain herself any longer. The desire is dilating her pupils. Her cow-like eyes are moist. Perhaps she will ask me to call her mummy.

'Do you have a career?' Isobel asked.

'I am a teacher. I like working with children.'

'Aah,' said Isobel. 'I see.' Blooming on the sofa, she was voluptuous, understanding, smiling, benign. 'I understand,' she said. 'And now I must go up to bed.'

'Goodnight, darling,' said Valerie.

Isobel met her father at the foot of the stairs.

'What do you think?' he said.

'What about?'

'About her. About Valerie.'

'Oh. About her. I haven't really given her much thought.'

'Oh haven't you,' said Antony.

'She's motherly. She wants to mother me. She hasn't got a clue.'

Now she was pregnant Isobel changed the sheets on her bed every two or three days. The washing machine in the kitchen was endlessly churning. The drying machine gave off the manufactured cleanliness scent of washing powder.

The clean sheets were dry and stiff at first; the washed cotton roughly stroked her limbs and back and belly. Then the cotton absorbed moisture from her body and it became limp. The smoothness of limp sheets against her smooth skin was unpleasant so she stripped the bed and carried the dirty sheets downstairs to the kitchen in a bundle under her arm.

The anticipation of the virgin cotton loveliness of bedtime made her take a bath each night before retiring, so that her own cleanliness would increase the pleasure awaiting her. A clean nightgown, white, long-sleeved, buttoning up to the neck, was the proper attire.

The whiteness of the sheets and her nightgown enveloped her in a dream of childish innocence; she was a small female child, and a child was growing inside her. The roughness of the sheets stroked her skin in a dream of pure pleasure when her nightgown rode up. There was no need for a man in that bed for pleasure. Her own cleanness pleased her. It was herself that was making a baby. She was complete. There was no need for a man at all.

Eighteen

The bitch, extenuated by pain, her teats grossly swollen, the torn membranes of her vagina bleeding, lolls on a soiled blanket and shows her pale underbelly. She has eaten the nutritious afterbirth and now she sleeps.

Mr Green kneels to examine the puppies. There are a pair of puppies with their mother in the basket. Their eyes are still blinded by birth. One has only three legs. Its brother's head is malformed.

Mr Green bundles the puppies into a hold-all. He can hear them crying. Their whimpers are pitiful.

Buttoning up his coat to the neck Mr Green braves the searing winds of March that skin his face. The railwayland will be deserted. The puppies are wriggling in the hold-all, crying for their mother helplessly into the wind.

In the oil drum by the broken shed there is ice on the surface of the water. Mr Green breaks it with the sharp point of a stick. Then it is a question of whether to take the puppies out of the hold-all or not; to take them in his hands and immerse them in the freezing water and hold them under until they drown or to drown them in the bag. That would be to throw away a perfectly good bag. Except that they had probably dirtied it already in fright. Leaving them in the bag would be less unpleasant. He would not have to see them die.

Mr Green plunged the hold-all into the barrel and held it under the water until there were no more air bubbles rising out of it and then he let go. The bag sank slowly to the bottom of the drum and he withdrew his arm, his fingers stiff with cold. Fishing his handkerchief out of his trouser pocket he wiped himself and rolled down his sleeve.

Nineteen

Out of dead wood among dusty leaves in the hedge that gave cover to the blue house and caught litter on its twigs, new shoots bore shiny buds. The dusty leaves broke off and fell away; out of papery casings new leaves unfurled; now the hedge was dense with fresh foliage.

It was tea-time. Buttery biscuits were arranged on a white plate on the tea table and a white jug held daffodils, their folded trumpets showing yellow through split stamens. There was a melting smell in the room of baking.

Valerie was pouring the tea. Her cardigan, buttoned at the waist, gaped open over her chest, and as she leaned across the small table her breasts heaved out of the gap inside a voluminous blouse and her belt nipped her. Her feet were placed together side by side on the floor in patent court shoes.

'Neat ankles,' said Sylvia.

Norman caught her sly murmur and smiled. 'Pass me a biscuit,' he said.

Her own dress was slippery. Anemones, black and rose, bloomed on a purple ground, and the expanses of purple were sprinkled with yellow pollen.

'What a marvellous dress,' said Valerie. 'It's so unusual. Did you make it yourself?'

Sylvia was disarmed for an instant. Was this rudeness? Valerie's mouth quivered with smiles. It couldn't be.

'Norman bought it for me,' she said.

'How lovely,' said Valerie.

Antony handed round the biscuits, nodding faintly at his garish guests.

'Thank you,' said Sylvia.

'Thank you,' said Norman, comfortable by the fire in Antony's armchair.

Isobel was resting on the sofa, bolstered up by several cushions, a blanket around her shoulders. There was little room for anyone else on the sofa, and Isobel was cold. In the aching cavities of vertebrae and skull the cold was wandering, and a rattling chill embraced her. 'I'm cold,' she said.

'It's the baby,' said Sylvia.

'Yes,' said Valerie. 'You do get cold when the baby is coming.' She sipped her tea, leaning back and resting her saucer on her chest, and frowned, knowingly. 'Will they give you pethidine? Or an epidural?' she asked. 'The episiotomy nowadays is routine, you know.'

'And the enema,' said Sylvia. 'And they shave you. More hygienic. On the off-chance of complications,' she added.

Isobel was oblivious to their questions and warnings. 'Put some more coal on the fire, Dad,' she said.

'I bet it's a boy,' said Valerie.

'They say you can tell by the shape of the lump,' said Sylvia. 'Where will he sleep?'

Isobel shifted under her blanket. 'I don't know. In with me, I suppose.'

'That won't be any good,' said Sylvia. 'He'll turn out to be a right mummy's boy.'

Antony cleared his throat. 'I will move out of my study. I can move my desk and my books into my bedroom,' he said.

Isobel stared at him. He was giving up his study for the baby. He had never given up anything for her.

'I'll give the room a coat of paint,' he said.

'Thanks Dad,' said Isobel.

That sombre brown forbidden room out of which the ping and click of the typewriter incessantly rattled was to be thrown open. Finally those sacred piles of books and papers were to be disturbed. Her father was giving up his room for her baby. She would be able to enter at will without knocking and close the door on him. In the house he would wander, displaced, perhaps with some belongings in a carrier-bag, homeless as a refugee. Perhaps then he would cry. Out of that forbidden room he would hear the singing of lullabies. He would not be admitted.

'Well you'd better get a move on,' said Sylvia.

Isobel opened her mouth and whined. Her eyes closed, the lids puckering under drawn brows, and opened as she exhaled. Long and thin the breath came out of her chest. Grey discs of iris in her eyes blackened and her pupils dilated like the spread of spilt ink. Then the eyeballs rolled back in her head until the red-rimmed sockets were full of nothing but whiteness veined with red.

'Oh my God,' said Isobel.

Her head was moving aimlessly with pain. Antony and Norman stood up and shuffled their feet and coughed. Creeping towards her slowly as if anxious never to arrive at her side, their minute progress was blocked by the swooping advance of Sylvia and Valerie.

'Hold my hand,' said Isobel.

'Breathe deeply,' said Valerie.

Isobel felt their hot hands rubbing and kneading her. Out of the back of her head her huge black pupils rolled and she saw, hanging above her, the eager shoving faces of the two women, smirking with concern. From painted mouths dithering in powdery faces scented words escaped on pants of hot breath as if by accident, and drifted away without meaning. Isobel could not push the faces away because she was using both hands to hold on to her abdomen. In the chinks between ear and shoulder, elbow and side, Antony and Norman could be seen bending awkwardly towards her. Antony was tugging at his beard. Isobel looked at him through the gap between Valerie's breast and Sylvia's bottom. His face was shifty with embarrassment and fear. Then he began to shout.

'Leave her alone.'

Valerie and Sylvia retreated. The contraction subsided and Isobel grinned, weakly. 'It's coming,' she said.

Three-quarters of an hour later there was another contraction. Then the contractions came more frequently and stronger. Antony phoned for an ambulance. Sylvia and Valerie sat quietly together, under orders not to pester Isobel. Norman was in the kitchen making more tea.

There was no turning back now. The baby was going to come. The pain was swallowing inside her, swallowing her up. It gulped and swallowed until she was nothing, then let go of her and left her panting. And then it swallowed her again. She held out her hand and grasped at the air as if to save herself from going down. No one took the flailing hand. Her father was watching at the window for the ambulance. It was the baby that was hurting her.

'Hold me,' she cried. 'Hold my hand.'

Sylvia and Valerie looked at Antony. He turned and moved towards his moaning daughter. The pale hand flailed limply in the air. Antony took it and knelt at his daughter's side. The pain subsided.

'Come with me,' she said.

'If you want me to,' he said.

'I do. Please.'

'I will.'

The sun sank behind the turrets and castellations as they arrived at the hospital, casting long and gloomy shadows. The ambulance man was wearing spicy aftershave. His mouth smelled of peppermints. 'Easy does it,' he said, lowering Isobel into a wheelchair. 'Best not to walk in. You might fall over. Conserve your energies.'

'I'll push her,' said Antony.

'Take the lift. Fourth floor maternity,' said the ambulance man. 'Best of luck.'

Isobel's face was pale and frightened like the face of a child. Her father pushed her into the lift and hurried in after her.

'I'm scared,' said Isobel.

'Don't be scared,' said Antony. 'Nothing to it. Easy as pie.'

And then the pain swallowed again inside her and gulped and swallowed. The pain was a feeding monster sucking her into itself. She lost herself in the pit of its stomach. It digested her into itself and she was transmuted. She was the feeding monster, swallowing herself inside out. There was nothing but pain.

And then she was lying on a high hard bed. The monster was sleeping. The monster was her child. Her father was standing at the window, looking out at the night sky. Isobel realised that the hand she was holding did not belong to him. The hand smelled of carbolic soap. The monster awoke.

There were no gaps now in the pain. There was the pain of the womb contracting and the pain of the cervix dilating. The two pains became one. The nurse administered gas and air. A face peered round the door and disappeared. The midwife was talking. 'Push,' she said. 'Don't push.'

Antony was not in the room.

'Looking for your old man?' said the nurse. 'Don't worry. He's outside having a fag.'

There was nothing but pain. The midwife was fumbling about between Isobel's legs. 'That's your waters broken. Soon be all over,' she said.

That was when Isobel started to scream. She fought the nurse for gas and drew blood on her hand.

'Gas,' she screamed.

The gas disconnected her head. The pain remained. Isobel screamed.

'Easy,' said the midwife. 'Push. Don't push.'

Nothing could stop the pain. In Isobel's disconnected head the horror became clear suddenly; there was no way out. The pain would not go away. The pain was her baby hurting her. There was no bravery or aloofness. Isobel was helpless. The baby would never go away. The baby was coming.

'Push,' the midwife shouted. 'Push. Push.'

Isobel pushed. Her face was crimson and glistened with the sweat of fruitless effort. Her white thighs were taut.

'Push,' the midwife shouted.

Isobel pushed. Out of the gash of slit vagina the head of the baby appeared. The head was smeared with blood and mucus.

'Push, for God's sake,' said the midwife.

Isobel pushed.

'It's a girl,' said the midwife.

Isobel felt the small wet wriggling thing on her chest. She caught at it with weary arms fondly and it screamed. The midwife cut the cord and took it away.

Twenty

Where is my baby? There is a soapy milky smell in here, of zinc and castor oil cream B.P. and sick. The sick of the baby is mild and clean like milk. Oh there she is, a snoozing creature wrapped in white garments, lying on her side on the bed. Her tiny chest is rising and falling minutely and her lips are slippery. Rolls of flesh crease, a shower of fine powder silted up in the tiny folds to prevent chafing, and she strokes her wrinkled cheek with a sharp-nailed finger. On her face is a smattering of scarlet blemishes, raised lumps, pin-head spots – a rash. The baby has a rash on its face. The baby is exhaling from its nose. A small bubble forms at the nostril and bursts. This baby belongs to me. Its skull is as thin as eggshell. What is inside its head? Fine wispy hairs cover the scaly scalp and when she smiles she looks sweet. They say that the early smile is a sign not of pleasure but of indigestion. The smile makes her look babyish. When she smiles her face is puckered, chubby, undefined. She is unrecognisable. Then when she frowns her small eyebrows draw together and lend to her forehead a manly solidity and recognisable weightiness as of knowledge and desire. Her mouth is set in a silent gawp of reproach – she is getting at me – is she getting at me? And then she smiles again like a baby. I had anticipated a scream tearing out of that mouth but she declined to scream at me. She knows what she wants. She wants to smile like a baby. The frown she is saving to disarm me with later.

She looks like my father. My child is a monster. There are no two ways about it. Look at her monstrously grasping fingers scraping the skin off her face. I have tried to stop her. I have no scissors small enough to trim her fingernails. I tried to file them down with an emery board but she screamed. I tried to bite them off by putting the ends of her fingers into my mouth but she screamed. She's a little monster. She doesn't care about me. She couldn't give a damn about me. She screams when I pick her up and when I put her down. I keep on thinking I will get the hang of it but I don't. It's her fault. She won't let me. I thought babies were supposed to be vulnerable and fragile. My baby is robust. I'm sure that if I chucked her out of the window she would land on her feet. The first time I was alone with her she lay in my arms smiling at me and I cried like a baby. I felt as if she should be holding me. I am the motherless neglected vulnerable one. She's as tough as old boots. So I cried. I panic when she will not stop crying and I panic when she lies in my arms silently and gazes at me. I fill the vast gap of her silence with nightmare. I cannot leave her. I am stuck with her. What have I done? She looks at me with her clever curious eyes as if to forgive me. If she could speak I know what she would say. She would say 'You haven't got a clue.'

Then out of the folds and creases of her chin and chubby cheeks a smile emerges, trusting and babyish, and my wasting black panic effervesces. I do not recognise her. Whose baby is this anyway? I try to smile at it but my lips are caught up against my teeth. She is fragile now. Is this better or worse? I think that it is worse. And yet my panic subsides. Now I am merely flatly grimly anxious. That's not too bad. The baby is gurgling. That is as it should be. Now she needs me. I can bear it. I have no choice.

Do I enjoy it? The baby is sleeping. I would like to flush it down the lavatory and pull the chain. Then I would be free. A small frail hand clenches and uncurls, the fingers small and perfectly formed, and I bend to gather my baby up from the bed to my chest. Poor little soul. She begins to scream. The gummy toothless gob opened cavernously in the small round head and let out a shriek. I stared transfixed down the throat of my baby and saw the silvery epiglottis trembling. It was my baby that purpled sodden struggling thing. I threw it down on the bed in despair. I tried to talk to it. 'What do you want my darling?' I said in a soothing voice. 'What is the matter my little one?' And still it screamed. It would pause for breath, gasp, and scream again. 'Ssh,' I whispered. The baby's face was soaked with tears, running snot and spit. I tried to wipe it with a piece of cotton wool but she screamed with still more vigour and began to choke. The ward sister had told me to leave it when it cried or I would spoil it. I could not leave it. I screamed at it. That didn't make any difference. I tried naming her; it was difficult to make myself heard above the bellowing but I tried. 'Fiona,' I said. 'Fiona.' I got the idea to call her Fiona from Sylvia. The name seems to me to hold some promise. I thought that if I reminded the screaming child of her name she might quieten. Of course I was mistaken. There was a pause in her effort to deny her own helpless weakness, a pause momentarily in her effort to vocalise her own power, as if she were listening to me, and then she continued to scream. I was surprised that such a small baby could make so much noise. I had imagined that the decibel level of a child would be in keeping with its size. And it was not just the amount of noise. Her scream contained within its stupid vastness a howl of knowing agony. My baby surely did have a reason to scream. She knew what was what. Again I lifted her off the bed and held her to my chest. It was almost unbearable to feel her mouth so close to my ear. The scream was lacerating – I endured the shredding of my eardrums.

99

Unbuttoning the front of my shirt I fumbled with stiff nylon and elastic to release one bloated breast out of its cup. I tried to stick the raw nipple into Fiona's mouth but she turned away. She did not want to drink my milk. She turned away in disgust. I squeezed the wriggling thing firmly in my arms to prevent it from escaping. In the struggle I felt its nails clawing at me. Its back was rigid with anger. It was clear that my baby did not like me. I was not surprised. Then I tried to kiss her. I pecked at her swollen eyelids with dry lips and cooing I pressed my lips into the gaping wet redness of her mouth. If she had teeth she would bite me. It would have been easy to seal up her mouth with the palm of my hand and smother her screams permanently, but I didn't want to silence her. I wanted to make her laugh. Or at least to make her smile. I sang her a song but still she would not smile at me. My squeezing and kissing and singing only made her more angry. I was unable to wipe that gawp off her face. She was unmoved by my efforts. I wanted her to gurgle and grin but she was too clever. She knew what was what and so she screamed. I could take no more. I screamed for my father. We needed help because we could not stop screaming. My father quietened us. He took my baby in his arms and she smiled at him. The baby began to gurgle. I saw them smiling at each other stupidly. It was clear that my baby liked my father. He was singing to her. You shall have a fishy on a little dishy. She liked him more than she liked me. It was clear that my father liked the baby. He liked her more than he liked me.

Twenty-one

Norman, shirtless and beaming, pushed the chromed and coach-built pram into the railwayland. The baby was tucked up under a fluffy blanket, yellow, white and powder-blue. A thin pillow bordered with broderie anglaise frills framed the baby's little face. A series of pastel-coloured plastic balls interspersed with pearly plastic ducks and rabbits were strung on elastic across the hood of the pram. Norman rattled these playthings as he manoeuvred the pram across wasteground where the air was laden with itchy pollen and dust, and sang.

> Green and yellow, green and yellow
> Oh mother come quick because I feel quite sick
> And I want to lay down and die.

The baby held out her chubby hands to Norman.

'Come to Daddy,' he said, sticking his head under the hood of the pram. 'Come on darling.'

He lifted her up, sat down in the long grass, and swung her in the air above his head. 'Weee! Weee!'

Fiona laughed. Norman lay her down in his lap and rummaged in the duffle-bag hanging off the handle of the pram for her bottle. Testing the temperature of the milk on the inside of his wrist and nodding to himself, he stuck the teat into Fiona's mouth.

A tiny creature, hard-shelled and shiny, crawled out of the grass and settled on Norman. He flicked it away with his forefinger, unsure whether the blow would kill it or stun it. 'Hello Fiona,' he said, grinning at his daughter. 'What a lovely baby. Just like your mother.'

The baby was sleeping after her feed.

Those eels were snakes my son,
My son Henry,
Those eels were snakes my son,
Henry my son.
Oh mother come quick because I feel quite sick
And I want to lay down and die.

Norman stroked the forehead of the sleeping baby. She was wearing a frilly bonnet to protect her from the sun. 'Where is your mother? She's gone to the shops to get some food for you. And where is my mother?' Norman bent his golden head and kissed the baby on her eyelid. 'My mother has gone out with Mr Green.'

What colour flowers my son?
My son Henry,
What colour flowers my son?
Henry my son.
Green and yellow, green and yellow.

'Mr Green is a dirty old bastard.' Norman extended one finger gently and touched Fiona on the mouth.

Oh mother come quick because I feel quite sick
And I want to lay down and die.

Twenty-two

The fire is on in the bathroom to create a cosy warmth for Fiona's bathtime. The blue baby-bath stands on its own folding legs at a convenient height so that bathtime is easy and safe. Isobel eases Fiona out of her stretch towelling suit and takes off her nappy. The grubby baby is patient and quiet. The bath is full of lukewarm water. Isobel carefully immerses the baby, supporting her head in the palm of her hand. The wet baby is slippery. She moves her legs and arms in the water because the stroke of the substance is pleasing. Isobel's fingers work under the water nimbly to remove dirt. When the baby is clean she is wrapped in a clean towel and carried away into the nursery.

The nursery is warm and well-appointed. The walls are painted yellow, a sunny colour recommended by Sylvia for its cheerful effect, and at the window hangs a pair of curtains, made by Valerie, sky-blue to match the new carpet. The cot is sturdy, made of wood, once slept in by the infant Isobel.

Fiona lay on her back on the changing-mat, pink and shiny after her bath, and grizzled, waving her small hands in the air.

'Sssh now darling,' said Isobel, smearing cream on to Fiona's bottom. 'There's a good girl,' she said, sprinkling powder over the wriggling child. 'Who's a little angel?'

Isobel fastened a nappy round Fiona's chubby little middle and dressed her for bed. 'Let's sit by the fire.'

Fiona's bottle was keeping warm in a basin of hot water. Isobel fished it out and dried it on the skirt of her apron. 'Here's your nice milk. Open your little lips.' Fiona opened her lips and drank. 'Time for bed now,' said Isobel, lowering the sleeping baby into her cot. Fiona settled on her side and began to breathe evenly. 'Goodnight, darling,' said Isobel, and crept out of the room.

Tiptoeing across the landing Isobel withstood the desire to reopen the nursery door and return to her sleeping child. There was the pull of sweet breath making the darkness fragrant and the stillness to be resisted because the child must sleep. It was no good her creeping about in the shadows of the nursery like a ghost. The child must be left in peace.

A dull ache stiffened in the muscles and tendons of Isobel's legs and a prickling slackness drew her breasts downwards; the weight of her breasts rounded her shoulders and made her sigh; the night was hot after the long hot day.

Sinking into the softness of her bed Isobel swooned into numbness. The swoon was black and gorgeous like velvet or the midnight sea. There was blindness in the swoon, and deafness, yet sunk in oblivion one fact remained – the baby was sleeping in the same empty blackness.

Behind the wall that separates the mother and the child footsteps can be heard traversing the gap between the floor and the cot. A floorboard creaks and then there is a pause as if the intruder, standing on one leg, is waiting for a lapse of attention in the ear of the listener before proceeding.

Antony's voice, intonating languidly, passes through the plaster and the paper and the paint. His voice is expressive, soaring, grating, a buzz distorted by its passage, melodic, clear. Antony must have crept into the darkness and found the baby.

The wall disintegrated, its many coats of paint and layers of paper peeling away cleanly leaving crumbling naked brick, and collapses. The child and the mother are undivided. Is that a considerate stifled footstep skittering across the nursery floor? Who is playing with my baby?

The numb black swoon is peopled with shadows by sleep. The blind eye and the deaf ear are peeled and cocked to dream. Under cover of night, his shoes stealthily removed, a mess of moist dirt rubbed into the pores of his pale face to stop it from shining in the dark and scaring the baby, a man leans over the cot. The man is holding his breath in his chest and inside his hood his streaked face is owlish. A mildewed cloak enfolds him. He lifts the sleeping infant from her bed and presses her to his lips. His tongue pokes out of his bearded face and he is panting like a dog. His tongue stiffens, gleaming in the dark, and insinuates itself into the baby's mouth. Then the tongue is withdrawn. It hangs limply, stretching out under its own weight, and flaps against the bearded chin. The man extends it, tugging at it with his fingers until it reaches full length, and wipes its warty surface across the baby's cheeks and forehead. A voice penetrates Isobel's head, dislodging a vestige of dream that flees when she wakes leaving nothing but wretchedness blinking into the dark where the wall stands solid four inches in front of her nose.

She raises herself in the bed and presses her ear to the wall to ascertain whether the melodic buzz is a song of sleep or waking. Now the voice is strong and soaring, piecing together a recollection or stain in her head of the dream that she grasps at before it eludes her. The song exists outside her dull head; it is not of her imagining; her father is singing.

Rosy lips upon the water
Blowing bubbles mighty fine
But alas I was no swimmer
And so I lost my Clementine.

Isobel climbed out of bed.

How I missed her, how I missed her
How I missed my Clementine

Hesitating barefoot in her nightgown and trembling she waited for the conclusion of the song.

So I kissed her little sister
And I forgot my Clementine.
Oh my darling, oh my darling,
    oh my darling Clementine
Thou art lost and gone for ever
Dreadful sorry Clementine.

Isobel ran out of her room and opened the door of the nursery. In the gleams and shadows she made out the ungainly bulk of her father hanging over the side of the cot. He jerked upright as she entered. 'I heard her whimpering, so I came in to soothe her,' he said.

'Liar,' said Isobel.

Antony looked at her with widening eyes.

'What are you doing with my baby?'

'I am singing her to sleep.'

'Get out,' Isobel hissed. 'Leave her alone. She needs to be left alone in peace to sleep.'

'I couldn't resist it,' said Antony jovially. 'She's such a little darling.'

'Oh is she?' said Isobel. 'Since when have you been so keen on babies?'

'I am not keen on babies. I'm keen on Fiona.'

Isobel looked at his beaming face. 'I bet you weren't keen on me when I was a baby,' she said.

'No, I was not,' said Antony.

'Well?'

'Well what?'

'So what's so good about her?'

'She's not mine,' said Antony.

They returned to their rooms in gloomy silence and left the baby alone.

Twenty-three

It was a perfect afternoon for a walk. Sylvia, dressed in a mauve two-piece of shiny cloth with pearl buttons that matched the new string of pearls she wore around her neck, caught the hand of Mr Green (the hand that had presented her with the pearls in their little velvety presentation box lined with black satin) and pressed it to her lips. His nails were immaculately trimmed and his fingers gave off a mild fragrance of coal-tar soap.

'Don't you smell nice,' said Sylvia. 'Where's that dog of yours? Has she had her pups yet?'

'The dog is at home, convalescing. The pups were stillborn,' said Mr Green.

'What a shame. I fancied a little puppy myself,' said Sylvia. 'How has she taken it?' she asked.

'Who?'

'The dog. The bitch. Tiger or whatever you call her.'

'Oh Tiger. She's convalescing. She's all right.'

'Good. It might have upset her badly. The shock.'

'She's all right,' he said.

The afternoon was balmy and warm. Mr Green, tugging at the collar of his short-sleeved shirt, looked up from his sandalled feet and saw advancing towards him a young couple pushing a huge pram. The man sported a glorious suntan. Mr Green recognised him. It was Norman. That must be Isobel. And little Fiona in the pram.

'Halloo there,' Mr Green called out.

'Hello,' said Sylvia.

'Hello,' said Isobel.

'Hello,' said Norman to his mother. 'Where's your dog, Mr Green? A dog is a man's best friend.'

'My dog is at home. Recovering from an unfortunate experience.'

'I am sorry,' said Norman. 'I bet you are lost without your four-legged friend.'

'I manage,' said Mr Green.

'You manage? I bet you do. I see you have other friends to keep you company.'

'Norman!' Sylvia exclaimed.

'One bitch is as good as another,' said Norman, quietly, into the rubbery silken-haired orifice of Mr Green's ear.

'I'd love to see the baby,' said Mr Green.

He bent over the pram and stuck his head inside the hood. 'What a lovely baby,' he said.

'Love 'er,' said Sylvia.

'Don't wake her up please. I've just got her off to sleep,' said Isobel.

'Sorry I'm sure,' said Sylvia, pursing her lips. 'I am sorry,' she said miserably.

'I didn't mean to hurt your feelings,' said Isobel.

'My feelings! Don't worry yourself about my feelings. It's the baby I'm worried about. Just a word of advice. If you don't mind.' Sylvia glanced at Isobel to see if she looked as if she minded, and continued. 'Don't molly-coddle the baby. Don't smother her. Or she won't grow up properly.'

'Mother!' said Norman. 'Let Isobel get on with it. You haven't got a clue.'

'Well if you are going to take that attitude,' said Sylvia, folding her arms across her chest.

'Please mother, don't be horrible to me,' said Norman.

'Sorry son, ignore me, I'm a silly old woman,' said Sylvia.

Norman put his arm round his mother's shoulders and kissed her on both cheeks.

'I'm sorry,' she said. 'Don't mind me.'

'Shut up,' Norman shouted at her. It was the only way to stop her from going on. Her little moan petered out. 'What happens if she is molly-coddled?' he shouted. 'What happens if she is smothered?' There was a ghastly silence. Sylvia was crying inaudibly. 'What happens? I'll tell you. She will turn out like me.'

Mr Green was inspecting his neat fingernails. Sylvia was weeping loudly. Isobel grabbed Norman by the hand and drew him away. Fiona lay awake in her pram, staring up at her parents with wide eyes.

'You'll get over it,' said Isobel.

'I doubt it,' said Norman. He raised his fist to his face and bit at the knuckle of his forefinger. 'Can I come home with you?' His voice fell mumbling past the obstruction in the corner of his mouth. 'I can't face going home. I hate Mr Green.'

'Why?'

'Should I love him? I want to murder him.'

'Better to get rid of your mother.'

'Never.'

'Figuratively speaking,' said Isobel.

'I want to kill Mr Green.'

Fiona was asleep in her pram in the hall. Isobel was sterilising bottles. Norman stared at his tea until it went cold.

'Mr Green is not the point,' said Isobel. 'He is the least of your worries.'

'He would be if I got rid of him.'

'Then what would happen?'

'Mother would come back to me.'

'And what about Mr White and Mr Brown and Mr Yellow?'

'Is my mother a slag?'

'I am trying to explain to you that there are plenty more where Mr Green came from. Your mother wants a man.'

'She's got me. I'm going to kill him.'

'Forget it, Norman,' said Isobel.

Antony and Valerie bundled into the kitchen. 'I am going to take Fiona for a walk round the block,' said Antony. 'She needs fresh air. See you later.' Antony manoeuvred the pram out of the hall into the sunshine.

'No one asks me,' said Isobel.

'Don't you mind about old mother big tits?' Norman asked.

'She won't last. You'll see,' said Isobel. 'Nothing worth upsetting myself about. She'll leave him. They always do. It doesn't bother me. They are all old with big tits. I reckon the beard puts the young ones off.'

'Why do they all leave him?' Norman asked.

'I don't know,' said Isobel, rubbing her hands together.

'What do you do to them?'

'Nothing. Nothing special. I'm just myself.'

'Maybe I should try that,' said Norman.

Antony and Valerie returned with the baby and parked the pram in the hall. The inelegant racket of their eager footsteps could be heard in the kitchen as they thundered up the stairs.

'Maybe they are going upstairs to make a baby of their own,' said Norman.

'She's too old. She told me. There's no fear of that,' said Isobel.

Sylvia popped her head round the door. 'Hello dear. Hello Norman. You all right?' she said.

'Yes thanks,' said Isobel.

'That's nice. Just popped in. I'll be going then. Leave you two young people alone. Ta ta.'

'See you later,' said Norman, pulling a lugubrious face

and sheepishly backing out of the kitchen to follow his mother.

Isobel switched on the iron and set up the ironing-board. The laundry basket was full of small clean crumpled things. Methodically she smoothed and pressed and folded. The heat of the iron drew a homely smell out of the baby clothes. The work made her shoulders ache. Her breasts weighed heavily on her. Two wet patches darkened the pale cloth of her dress because milk was seeping out from her nipples. The fat red nipples were damp and sore. Perhaps Fiona was awake. It would be silly to wake her but only the ferocious sucking of those little lips could soothe the ballooning discomfort. The bursting tautness was unendurable. Isobel went to the hall and bent over the pram.

The longing to feel Fiona's fervent lips encircle her nipple and suck made her clumsy; she tore at the front of her dress, fumbling with the fastening of her sodden bra, and scooped out of the straining fabric one moon-like blue-veined breast. The baby smelled milk and sucked.

Twenty-four

'Mr Green is coming to tea,' said Sylvia. 'He knocks off early on Fridays like I do. The office shuts at three o'clock so as the boss can get away to the country. Miss the traffic. You know. A weekend cottage.'

'Nice,' said Norman. 'Is Mr Green bringing his dog?'

'Of course.'

'Good.'

'It's so nice you've grown attached to that animal,' said Sylvia.

'Which animal?'

'Very funny, Norman. Try and be nice dear. Oh there's the door. Do try and be nice Norman.'

The dog, a roly-poly docile bitch with a bristling coat, came sniffing and waddling into the front room on short little legs, wagging its tail and dribbling strands of spittle from its open mouth.

'Here Tiger,' said Norman, patting the gap on the sofa beside him. The dog obeyed. 'There's a good dog,' he said.

'Hello,' said Mr Green.

Norman was teasing the dog. The dog was yapping.

'Say hello to Martin,' said Sylvia.

'Hello Martin,' said Norman. 'Can I take Tiger out for a walk?'

'Certainly. I have her lead here somewhere.' Mr Green fished about in his pockets. 'Here we are,' he said, producing from inside his coat a leather strap joined at one end to a length of chain. The dog did not wear a collar. It began to pant as the chain rattled in Mr Green's hands. 'Walkies,' he said. The dog leapt off the sofa and offered up its neck to Mr Green. 'You have to thread this end of the lead through this ring to make a loop of chain and slip it over her head,' he explained. 'It strangles her if she tries to run away.'

'Very handy,' said Norman.

'There we are,' said Mr Green.

'See you later,' said Norman, leading the dog to the door.

The dog was unable to move quickly. It was as if carrying the weight of her own body was too much for her poor little legs. Out came the tongue, thick and stinking, to loll between her lower incisors, and straining out of her fat head her mournful yellow eyes rolled. Norman adjusted his pace patiently so that the little animal could keep up with him; the panting bitch followed on behind.

Outside the corner shop Tiger dawdled by the stained base of a lamp post and sniffed. Norman jerked at the lead, trying to make her follow, but she lingered. 'Come on Tiger,' he called. The lead was taut between dog and man. 'Move,' Norman shouted.

In the traces of piss and shit dried out at the bottom of the lamp post there was an ineluctable lure, an irresistible anamnesis breeding desire that petrified; the little bitch was unable to move.

'Tiger,' Norman shouted. The chain was tight round Tiger's neck. Norman pulled at the lead. The dog whimpered with discomfort but still she would not follow. Norman jerked the lead. The dog's paws scraped across the pavement as he dragged her away from the lamp post

114

and the chain round her neck loosened. Once she was away from the scent of dog the hold on her was broken.

'Come on Tiger,' said Norman.

Tiger followed on behind.

There was little pleasure for Norman in walking so slowly; he was unaccustomed to curtailing the power in his legs; the waddling dog had reduced him to shuffling; his patience was protracted. To swing his free arm squandered some of the unsprung kinesis in him, and yet, hampered by the little dog, he was bitten by an urgent longing to gallop. The meanness of the dog's idling spurred him to irritation; to run would be to strangle the dog; he wanted to strangle the dog. Norman increased his pace. The dog gasped behind him as the chain caught at her throat.

'Come on Tiger,' Norman shouted.

Strangulation and the effort to reduce the gap between itself and Norman made the dog whine. Its whining and gasping exasperated Norman. The greater the effort it made to keep up, the more it whined. The more it whined, the greater became Norman's desire to run. The faster it moved its little legs, the faster Norman walked. The distance between man and dog was only extendable by the reduction of the length of the chain encircling Tiger's neck. The more it whined, the greater became Norman's desire to run away from it. The faster Norman moved, the more it whined. For Norman to increase the gap between himself and the dog cost the dog inches. The dog emitted from its strangled throat a forlorn cry and abandoned its attempt to keep up. Under the weight of its roly-poly body the little legs splayed and collapsed and it hung by the neck on the end of the strap and screamed as Norman dragged it into the railwayland.

Once under the shadow of a plane tree that spread its branches magnificently over scrubland and dump, Norman released the animal and breathed easily in the gloom. Leaning against the trunk of the massive tree he smoked a cigarette and watched the dog nose about in the rubbish and weeds. The desire to run had left him. The dog was moving further and further away across the waste ground towards the gleaming railway-track.

Above Norman's head an agitating drift of dancing gnats or midges hummed in the air. A kestrel hung in the clear sky and scanned the dump with sharp eyes for prey. The little dog had disappeared. The absence of the little dog began to grate. Norman called to her.

'Tiger,' he shouted.

He searched in the brambles under peeling hoardings and found nothing but an old pair of shoes. He stirred cold water in an oil drum with a stick and found nothing but a bloated hold-all that he lifted out of the water, dripping and stinking.

Then in the patch of long grass where he had fucked Isobel amongst others because it made a change from wanking, and each time he laid in the grass warming his skin in the sunshine the smell of the grass and the heat reminded him of the time before and his penis began to stir (they never said no), behind the shed where he had seen his mother with Mr Green (that was what the long grass reminded him of now), in the long grass behind the shed he saw Tiger quivering under the weight of a large black alsatian – the dogs were stuck together fucking in the long grass.

Norman crept up behind the coupled dogs until he was close enough to smell their pleasure and screamed. His scream separated them. The alsatian sloped off into the scrubland wagging his tail.

Tiger lay panting on her back in the grass with her legs in the air. Norman crouched down and slipped the noose of the chain round her neck. He picked up the trembling dog, feeling the warmth of her damp sides against his chest, and carried her to the tree.

Holding her above his head by the folds of skin at the back of her neck he reached up with his other hand and flung the end of the lead over a branch. Twisting the end of the lead round his hand he let go of the dog and watched it dangle and writhe. The chain tightened round its neck and its eyes bulged. The dog was unable to bark or whine or gasp. Norman watched the piss and shit and come trickle out of its orifices and spill on to the ground. That was it. The dog was dead. Norman let go of the lead and as he ran he heard the dull thud of the roly-poly body hitting the earth.

Twenty-five

It was peaceful in the kitchen of the blue house. Fiona drank and dribbled, draining the rich milk out of Isobel's breasts until mother and child were stupid with soothing, and then she slept. Isobel laid her down in her pram in the hall and wandered into the kitchen to stare out of the window at the sunbeams caught in the dusty hedge. In the quietness there was a moment of vacancy perfect for melancholy thought. Isobel gazed at the shimmering hedge through wet eyelashes and out of the edge of her shiny eyes she saw the long brown figure of Norman scooting by through the gaps in the hedge. A spillage of tears washed thought from her head and she filled the moment with weeping.

Isobel did not raise a hand to her face to hide the shifting of her lips in grief – her crying was shameless. She did not hug her thin shoulders in the pitiful embrace of her own arms to offer herself comfort or crouch in an attitude of brokenness, holding her misery to herself. As the water dripped from her eyes she stood erect and gawped blindly in silence out of the window.

At last, from above, the gurgle and hiss of the lavatory

cistern and the singing of air in pipes heralded the descent of her father. It commenced immediately with the shuffle of slippers on the stairs. Of course the neat tap tap of sling-back sandals followed on behind. Valerie's laugh was gorgeously fruity because she had been fucked and fucked and fucked again.

Isobel found it difficult to produce an appropriate noise. A scream would be out of place here. A strangled whimper or swallowed wail of brave restraint would be more suitable. It was not a question of opening her mouth because her mouth was already open. She managed to squeeze out a feeble squeak, a laughable noise, tiny, and this shrunken sign of her grief made her so furious that she groaned. Then she caught hold of this groan as it rose in her throat, shaped it with her tongue, sharpened it inside her mouth, and it slipped out, just as her father and Valerie entered the kitchen, perfectly. She turned to show them her wet face.

'What on earth is the matter with you?' said Antony, strapping himself up round the middle with a leather belt.

Isobel continued to moan.

'Well?' he demanded.

Valerie bustled past him clothed in a voluminous shirt dress and tried to enfold Isobel in her arms.

'Please don't touch me,' gasped Isobel. 'I can't bear it. I can't bear it,' she wailed.

Valerie's arms, outstretched eagerly for embrace, fell uselessly and hung by her sides.

'Stupid woman,' Antony shouted. 'Leave my daughter alone. Sit down and shut up. Leave this to me.'

Valerie sat down heavily on the cold hard seat of a kitchen chair.

'Come on Isobel. What's the matter?' said Antony.

Isobel sobbed and sniffed. 'Don't be cruel to me, father,' she whispered.

Antony stared at her.

'Don't be cruel to me,' said Isobel in a small voice.

Antony looked at her carefully and waited.

'I can't bear it,' said Isobel, smiling bravely.

Antony sighed. Fiona began to cry.

'I'll get the baby,' said Antony.

In his absence Isobel appealed to Valerie with a mournful glance.

'What is it dear?' asked Valerie.

'He neglects me. He is cruel to me. He does not love me,' said Isobel.

Antony returned carrying Fiona, who was sleeping in his arms.

'He doesn't understand,' said Isobel.

'What don't I understand?' Antony shouted.

'It's about time you faced up to your responsibilities,' said Valerie.

'I beg your pardon,' said Antony.

'It's about time you faced up to your responsibilities. As a father,' she said.

'Oh really. I see. I thought I told you not to interfere. Why don't you mind your own business? You have no children of your own. What do you know you fat meddling bitch?'

Valerie lumbered to her feet and turned her back on Antony. 'I'm sorry, my dear,' she said to Isobel. 'I can't stay to be insulted. Your father is childish and unpleasant.' She kissed Isobel tenderly on the forehead. 'Goodbye, my dear,' she said. 'Perhaps you can change him.'

'Where are you going?' asked Antony. 'I'm sorry. I'm so sorry. Don't leave. Please.'

'I must go,' said Valerie, facing him with her arms folded across her bosom.

'Why?'

'For Isobel's sake,' said Valerie, and clattered out of the room.

'She has left me for your sake,' said Antony.

The front door slammed.

'I'm sorry,' said Isobel.

'They all leave me for your sake.'

'Do they?'

'Yes they do.'

'I'm sorry.'

Fiona muttered sweetly in Antony's arms. 'Left holding the baby,' he said.

'It's my baby,' said Isobel.

'Your mother left me holding the baby. You look just like your mother,' said Antony.

'I'm sorry,' said Isobel.

'No,' said Antony. 'I'm sorry. I must make amends.'

Isobel raised her big blue eyes to him. Her eyes shone with hope.

'I must make amends, I must be kind,' he said.

Isobel smiled at him encouragingly.

'I must be kind to the baby.'

Twenty-six

It was getting dark. A dry rustling and the snap of twigs
brought Isobel to the window. In the gloom between house
and hedge where the grass would not grow and dead leaves
mouldered a dark shape was crouching. Isobel tapped on
the window and saw a shifting of shadow on shadow: folds
of dark clothing and the darkening furls of dusk were
enfolded together. There were no outlines or edges. She
opened the window and called out softly into the night.
A voice answered from below, close to the ground, out of
the darkness.

'It's me.'

'Come in.'

It was Norman.

A smudged face loomed out from under the hedge. A
limp hand showed pale against the soil. Norman dragged
himself along on his hands and knees like a dying animal
and collapsed on the doorstep.

'Come in, come and say hello to Fiona,' said Isobel,
opening the door.

She looked down and saw the weeping man come rolling
into the hall.

'Come on. Get up,' she said, prodding him with her foot.

He lay as if dead. Isobel squatted beside him and pinched him gently on the back of his neck. She knelt over him and kissed the knuckle of his clenched fist. She embraced his stiff shoulders and whispered persuasively into his ear. The knot of flesh and bones loosened. Norman stretched his limbs and stood up. His face was smeared with chocolate. The brownness round his mouth was dark, like blood.

'Thanks,' he said.

'Come into the kitchen and have a cup of tea. I'll put the kettle on,' said Isobel.

'Da da,' said Fiona, sitting in her high-chair bashing the bottom of a tin plate with a spoon.

Slipping a muddy hand inside the front of his buttoned cardigan Norman pawed at himself and scratched the smooth skin of his chest and throat. His shoulders were hunched and lop-sided and his head wobbled on the end of his neck as if unhinged.

'I want to go to the toilet,' he said.

'Go on then. You know where it is.'

Norman hopped from one leg to the other and shuffled his feet. This spate of fruitless little jerks brought him no further to his destination.

'Go on,' said Isobel, arranging an assortment of iced biscuits carefully on a small plate.

Norman stood on one leg and stared at her. Perhaps unable to face the big giving glance he might meet in her eyes or to take the offer of love suggested in the persuasive whisper with which she had raised him from the floor he stared not at her face but at her breasts. Or could it be that if he met her eye to eye in that kitchen he would see that the whisper was a trick? The words had slithered out between her lips like a silvery caress. Was it her breath or her tongue that had moistened the silvery hairs on his ear lobe? Now she was pouring water deftly into the pot. Maybe he was mistaken. What were those words that had made him rise so swiftly from the floor? He could not remember. They had slipped away. Was it a trick to use words that dissolved? Under scrutiny they had evaporated. And yet moisture, their residue, pearled his ear lobe as evidence; that was certainly undeniable; the residue remained like a stain.

'Go on, get a move on,' said Isobel.

Norman mounted the stairs rapidly, leaping from tread to tread like a child. In the bathroom he wiped his face with a flannel and smelled in its sodden weave the sourness of old soap and sweat. The lavatory bowl was white and smelled of bleach. Norman unzipped his flies and released from inside his underpants his stiff penis. It was difficult for him to piss because of his erection. He pressed his penis down with his hand. 'Down boy,' he muttered, tapping the penis on the head with his forefinger. The piss trickled out slowly and made him sigh. It would be unbearable to shove his erect penis back into his trousers. Norman waggled it over the lavatory bowl between forefinger and thumb to shake off a droplet beading the eye. Then he dithered in the bathroom, from bath-tub to basin, from basin to bath-tub, watching his penis bobbing before him. He could hear Isobel calling him.

'Tea's ready! Come on Norman.'

He descended the stairs noiselessly and tiptoed into the kitchen. Isobel had her back to him. She was rinsing the tea-strainer under a gushing tap. The silvery splash of water reminded Norman of her whispered words. What was it she had whispered? Come to me? Come to me. Was that Isobel calling him? He jumped on her back and she crumpled beneath him.

'Get off me,' she giggled.

They tumbled together on the floor. Norman rolled her on to her back. Isobel gasped when she saw his swollen penis tilting at her.

'Norman,' she hissed. 'Put it away.'

Norman stared at her breasts.

'I love you,' he said.

'Shut up,' said Isobel. 'Leave me alone.'

Norman leapt on her and straddled her chest with his legs. She was pinned to the floor. The dancing penis swung in her face.

'Get off me,' said Isobel, turning her head away.

Norman caught at her hair and held her head still. 'Look at me,' he said.

Isobel closed her eyes firmly against him. Norman brushed her lips with the tip of his penis. The tip was faintly sticky. His touch was gentle like the stroke of a fingertip. The grim tautness of Isobel's face slackened.

'There, that's better,' said Norman.

Isobel opened her eyes. 'Get off me,' she shrieked. The eye of his penis was staring at her. 'I mean it Norman,' she said. 'Fuck off. Fuck off mummy's boy.'

'Don't,' said Norman. The rubbery florid erection wilted away.

'Thank God for that,' said Isobel, pushing his limp body off her onto the floor. Norman rolled under the kitchen table and sobbed. Isobel stood up. 'Come on, pull yourself together,' she said.

'I can't,' Norman wailed. 'I killed Mr Green's dog.'

Having spoken, Norman listened to the blurted words reverberating in his head without the relief of confession. There was no sense of having got the events of that dismal autumn afternoon off his chest. His words did nothing to shift the weight of nameless dread pinning him to the floor. Unable to move, he stuck his knuckle into his mouth and worked at the skin with his teeth. Isobel said nothing.

It was hard to convince himself that he had committed such an act. If only he could feel like a man who had killed. And particularly as the victim was only a dog. If only he could convert, with the strength of words, the weight on his chest to remorse. Remorse for a dog's life would be easy to bear. It was worth a try.

'I killed Mr Green's dog,' he repeated, accusing himself.

The words meant nothing. Neat formulation of his grief was denied him; there was nothing for it but to suffer messily under the table with his knuckle bitten between his teeth.

Fiona began to cry. Norman began to sob.

'Hello my darling,' Isobel cooed, lifting the baby out of her chair. 'Hello my little one. Who's a good girl then?'

'Da da,' said Fiona.

Isobel felt the shy stroking of Norman's fingers on her ankle. 'Come on Norman,' she said. 'Never mind about the dog. It's only a dog after all. It's not the end of the world. We'll talk about it later when you know who's in bed.'

'I killed it,' said Norman, mumbling from under the table.

'So you said.'

'On purpose,' he added.

'On purpose. I see,' said Isobel.

'Mr Green loves his dog. It was unpremeditated. I killed it on the spur of the moment.'

'Ah,' said Isobel. 'At least you didn't kill Mr Green.'

Norman crawled out of his hiding-place and stood up. His face was wet and fat with crying. He pushed his limp penis back into his trousers. 'Sorry,' he said, fumbling with the zip.

'What for?'

'For trying to rape you.'

'A rapist and a murderer! Don't be silly Norman. Sit down on that chair and keep quiet.'

'All right,' said Norman. 'It was you whispering. You gave me the idea.'

'Don't go on,' said Isobel, concentrating now on sprinkling Fiona's wiped bottom with baby powder. 'I bought her a new dress. Let's dress her up. It might take your mind off things.'

'All right,' said Norman.

Isobel took Fiona on her knee and bounced her up and down. Fiona shrieked.

'We'll make you beautiful for Daddy,' said Isobel, pulling the dress over the baby's head. 'Keep still darling. There's a good girl.'

'Can I put her socks on?' Norman asked.

Isobel handed them to him. They were trimmed with white lace that formed a ruff around Fiona's dimpled ankles.

'There,' said Norman. 'Who's a lovely girl then?'

Fiona smiled, her moist lips parting, and opened her big blue eyes.

'Isn't she a beauty?' said Norman, leaning towards the baby and peering into her face. 'She loves me! I can tell. See the way she is looking at me!'

'Oh Norman, you are a pain,' said Isobel.

'Why?'

'You only think about yourself.'

'That is not true,' said Norman, coldly.

Isobel held the baby out to him. 'Here, take her,' she said.

Norman stared at her.

'Take her!' Isobel raised her voice, thrust the child into Norman's lap and hurried across the kitchen towards the door.

'All right. Keep your hair on. Where are you going?'

'Out,' said Isobel. 'I need to breathe some fresh air and get out of this fucking house for ten seconds. I need to get away from you and that stupid baby and be on my own.'

Norman heard the front door slam.

'Mummy's going bonkers,' he said. 'Never mind. I'll look after you.'

Then Fiona began to cry. She opened her little mouth showing a single tooth and bawled until her face was scarlet. Beneath her puckered brow her eyes slitted, sank and disappeared. Blindly she screamed, bringing Antony down from his bedroom. She wailed, bringing Isobel in from the garden where she had been sieving the cool air of evening through her teeth.

'I'll make her some dinner. You look like you could do with some help,' said Antony.

Norman held the child out to Isobel. 'She wants you,' he said.

As soon as Fiona was calm and quiet Isobel slid her into the baby chair and sat down herself at the table beside Norman.

'You look tired,' said Antony.

'I am.'

Antony put the kettle on to boil and measured five spoonfuls of white powder out of a packet into a plastic dish. When the water had boiled he mixed a splash of it into the powder, stirring with a plastic fork. The paste he made was greenish, yellow streaked, flecked with red. 'Open wide,' said Antony, offering Fiona a spoonful.

Fiona opened her mouth, her tongue pointing out eagerly between her gums. Antony pushed the spoon into her mouth. She spluttered, expelling lumps of food on to the front of her dress. Isobel sighed. Antony scraped the splattered food off Fiona's chin with the side of the spoon and stuck it back into her mouth. She spat it out. 'Come on dear, there's a good girl,' said Antony. He scooped up a new spoonful of the food and pressed it into the baby's mouth. Fiona began to howl. She raised her hands to her mouth and smeared the greenish paste over her face. 'Fiona! Don't be a naughty girl,' said Antony. He loaded another spoon and forced it into the mouth of the crying baby. Fiona choked. The slippery mouthful seeped out of her nostrils. Antony removed it with the corner of a drying-up cloth. Fiona was screaming. Her skin and clothing were spread with cream of vegetable casserole that lent a greenish tinge to her rosy complexion. Antony dashed round the kitchen; his forehead was shining; a blob of baby food lodged on his beard. Clumsily he scraped the unwanted supper from the dish into the bin. He looked at Fiona and saw that she was screaming with hunger and anger. Norman was pulling faces at her in an attempt to be amusing. Isobel followed the movements of her father with her eyes. Antony threw open the fridge door and scanned its contents in desperation.

'Give her a yogurt, she likes that,' Norman suggested.

Antony tore the lid off the plastic container, breathing heavily. Fiona quietened. 'There you are,' he said, filling up her open mouth. Fiona gulped and held up her arms and opened her mouth for more.

When the baby was fed Antony lifted her out of the baby chair and held her gingerly away from his body. 'Say goodnight to Mummy,' he said. 'I'll give her a bath and put her to bed.'

'Thanks,' said Isobel.

'Goodnight,' said Norman. 'Sweet dreams.'

Isobel and Norman listened to the steady receding sweep of Antony's slippered feet on the stairs as he climbed with Fiona in his loving arms to the bathroom; they heard the tender solicitousness in his voice; and then the silver fall of water.

'What was it you whispered to me?' Norman asked. 'The words you whispered. They slipped away.'

'I can't remember. Shut up about it would you. Change the subject.'

'All right. All right. I will. What happened to Valerie?'

'She left him. I knew she would.'

'Why did she leave him?'

'For my sake, apparently.'

'Do you feel bad about it?'

'There are plenty more fish in the sea.'

'Anyway,' said Norman. 'I looked at my face in the mirror on Wednesday night when mother was at bingo and I'm sure I'm developing those flaps of hanging cheek like Mr Green. My tan has faded. There is a cap like his in the window of Dunn and Co. Mother said she would buy it for me. Will you buy it for me?'

'No I will not,' said Isobel.

'Why not?'

Isobel raised her hands to her face and used them to cover her eyes and mouth.

'Why not?' Norman demanded.

Into the soft red blackness of her palms Isobel bared her teeth and shed tears. She smelled on her skin the odour of potato peelings. The earthy smell was brown, bodily.

'Why not? Why not? Why not?'

Norman was insistent; he seemed to be chanting – his words were few and came too often. His little voice slipped into Isobel's ear and meandered in the blackness in her head; out of her squashed mouth between grinding teeth into the flesh of pressing palms she spoke.

'For fuck's sake Norman. What are you on about? I haven't got the answer. You are mad. I know how you feel. Give me a break. Look at me. I am crying.' She removed her hands from her face and lowered her head to avoid the startled pain in Norman's eyes. 'I am crying Norman because I am miserable. I am lonely, I'm tired, I'm miserable. I weep and my father makes amends to Fiona. I weep and you ask me to buy you a hat.' Sobbing swallowed up her words.

Norman stood up suddenly. 'Come here,' he said, smiling a beneficent handsome smile and holding out his big strong arms to Isobel. 'Come here my darling,' he said.

Still sobbing and hesitant Isobel moved with frailty like an old woman; she wiped her raw face on her sleeve, slipped into Norman's arms and let him hold her like a child.

'Come to me,' she said.

Twenty-seven

Biting insidious dampness and a silent wind carried Mr Green along the dirty street towards the house of his loved one, the skirt of his overcoat flapping. She would be waiting for him, her colour heightened by the heat of the fire, proffering cake and biscuits and hot tea against the cold.

His overcoat was buttoned up to the chin. In the breast pocket of his jacket was a small box, lined with padded satin, containing a plain gold ring, set with a single diamond, modest in size yet lit with blue fire. The ring was for Sylvia. It would look well on her. The fire was the colour of her eyes.

Mr Green depressed the button of the doorbell and blew into his cupped hands as the chimes sounded. He was unable to recognise the first few bars of a popular song. Sylvia opened the door.

'Come in. Come in.'

Mr Green kissed her quickly on the mouth.

'Take off your coat. Come and sit by the fire. You've brought the cold in with you. I'll put the kettle on.'

He heard her bustling about in the kitchen. Steam was

rising from his sodden shoes. The little box pressed on his chest. Sylvia was calling him.

'Would you like some cake? It's still warm from the oven.'

'Yes please,' said Mr Green, fishing the little box out of his jacket pocket. The box was small in the palm of his well-scrubbed hand.

When the tea was ready Sylvia kicked open the front-room door; Mr Green concealed the box in his sleeve; Sylvia placed the tray of tea things on a low table.

'Here,' she said, handing him a cup brimming with milky tea. She cut a fat slice of cake and flipped it on to a plate with the blade of the knife.

'Delicious,' said Mr Green.

He applied his lips to the rim of the cup carefully, anxious not to slurp. He ate his cake neatly with a fork, catching falling crumbs in his handkerchief. The little box was caught in the folds of lining and shirt inside his sleeve.

The moment was propitious. A small smile spread and stretched showing teeth in Sylvia's rosy face.

'Will you marry me?'

Mr Green set his cake plate down on the side of the tray, took a final sip of tea, and set his cup down on top of it.

'I have never been married,' said Sylvia.

'That is of no consequence. Neither have I.'

Mr Green stood up to shake the box out of his sleeve. It appeared in his hand as if by magic.

'For you,' he said.

Sylvia took the box and opened it. The ring was beautiful. Mr Green knelt suddenly at her feet.

'Marry me,' he said.

He pulled the ring out of its slit in the satin display cushion and slipped it on to Sylvia's finger.

'What about Norman?' she asked.

'What about Norman?' said Mr Green. 'You can't let him run our lives. We've had this conversation before. If necessary I will talk to him man to man. There will be no more pranks. Norman will understand.'

'Do you think so?'

'I do. Will you marry me?'

'I will. I'll call Norman.'

They were sitting side by side on the sofa slightly apart, as if to belie the announcement they were about to make when Norman entered the room.

'Sit down, son,' said Sylvia. 'I have something to tell you.'

Norman sat down in the armchair where his mother had been sitting and turned towards her, smiling and raising his eyebrows interrogatively.

'Norman, Mr Green and I are to be married.'

'How nice,' said Norman.

Sylvia showed him the ring.

'How nice,' he said.

'We were worried that you would be put out, weren't we dear?' said Mr Green, reaching for Sylvia's hand.

'Yes we were,' said Sylvia.

Norman laughed, closing his eyes and passing the back of his hand softly across his forehead. 'Me?' he said. 'Don't be absurd. I am happy for you. I am truly happy for you both. Congratulations. Congratulations and jubilations.'

'Thank you,' said Sylvia.

'Thank you,' said Mr Green.

Norman, graceful and beaming, bowed out of the room.

'See,' said Mr Green.

His familiar tweed was hanging, one sleeve turned inside out, the lining split on the seam to show the construction of the armhole, on a coat-hook in the hall. Beneath it was Norman's camel-hair coat, a present from Sylvia, sharing the same peg. Norman extricated it, smoothing the sumptuous cloth with the flat of his hand, and slipped it on. The embrace of the coat was light and reassuring. Norman opened the front door. Refuse and dead leaves spun in the gutter and the awning of the corner shop billowed. In the high street women shrieked and held down their skirts. A broken umbrella whipped across the pavement, an elbow of bent spoke poking through gashed nylon. Lifted on wings of flapping black it soared above the heads of passers-by and then it fell under the wheels of an oncoming vehicle and was flattened.

Warm air spangled with a dusting of translucent powder wafted from the parfumerie and engulfed Norman as he entered the department store.

The pressure of his cold feet was absorbed into the carpet silently and a display of trailing scarves stroked his cheeks as he walked in the aisles through the crowds between counters where, under golden lamps, luxury items were arranged to catch the eye. A woman sprayed the back of his neck with aftershave and the wet patch cooled him as it dried. He bought some initialled linen handkerchiefs folded and ribboned in a tartan box. The fingers of the assistant touched his palm as she gave him change. He bought a pair of swansdown slippers in a transparent vinyl travelling case, a rose made of black silk, a five-year diary fitted with a tiny padlock, and a painted glass giraffe. Then, as he lingered in the foyer, his arms full of small packages, bracing himself to face the cold in his camel coat, he saw Isobel waving to him at the entrance to the lift.

'Come and have a cup of coffee,' said Isobel. 'In the buttery on the fourth floor. It's nice. Here's the lift.'

They rode up together in the small steel box.

'What a coincidence,' said Isobel. 'Christmas shopping?'

'No,' said Norman.

The lift stopped almost imperceptibly and the doors opened on to the cafeteria.

'Find a table. I'll go and queue. Would you like a cake?' said Norman.

'A chocolate éclair and a white coffee please.'

'Right you are.'

He queued and ordered. Isobel was sitting at a small table by the window. Norman piled his purchases on to the tray beside the coffee and carried it over to her.

'Where's Fiona?' he asked.

'At home with dad.'

'Will you marry me?'

'No I won't. You're always asking me that. I'll tell you if I change my mind.'

'Guess what?'

'What?'

'Mother is marrying Mr Green. Hence the shopping expedition. I've bought her some presents.'

'How nice,' said Isobel. 'How do you feel about it?'

'How do I feel? Calm and collected,' said Norman. 'Nice coffee,' he added, stirring the pale frothy liquid with the handle of a spoon. 'Nice cake.'

Isobel showed him the little vests she had bought for Fiona.

'How nice,' he said, gathering up his packages. 'I must dash.'

On the way home Isobel stopped at the florists to buy a bunch of flowers for Sylvia and Mr Green. Forced winter blooms gave off a green hygienic fragrance that mingled with the cold earth smell of potted ferns. She chose a bunch of dahlias, lemon and lime dahlias, the green eyes bleeding into yellow. Roses were too expensive. The florist wrapped the flowers in floral paper and Isobel tucked them under her arm.

'Hello,' said Sylvia as she opened the front door.

'I've heard the news,' said Isobel, holding out the bunch of flowers. 'Norman told me. Congratulations.'

Sylvia took the flowers. 'Lovely,' she said. 'Thank you. Come in. Take your coat off. Come and sit by the fire.'

Sylvia arranged the flowers in a cut-glass vase and put them on the mantelpiece. 'How did he seem?'

'Norman?'

'Yes.'

'He was all right I think. He's bound to be a bit difficult at first. I don't think he's too keen on Mr Green.'

'He's not being difficult,' said Sylvia. 'He offered us his congratulations. He smiled and congratulated us.'

'He would,' said Isobel.

'What are you getting at?'

'Nothing,' she said. 'It's just that I don't think he likes Mr Green very much.'

'Oh it's just jealousy,' said Sylvia. 'Not to worry. It'll pass.'

'I hope so,' said Isobel.

'So do I. At least he's making an effort.'

'An effort?'

'To be nice,' said Sylvia.

Isobel smiled at her. Sylvia smiled at Isobel. 'I want to show you a photograph,' she said. 'I'll fetch it. It's upstairs.'

Isobel warmed her hands at the fire.

'Look,' said Sylvia, coming back into the room holding a photograph by one corner. 'She's just like you!'

Isobel examined the picture and turned it over. There was an inscription written on the back in a trembling hand. "With all my love Fiona".

'Fiona,' said Isobel.

'She's so beautiful,' said Sylvia.

'Who is she?'

'I don't know.'

'Where did you get it from?'

'From my father.'

'Your father gave it to you?'

'No. I stole it out of his pocket.'

'Why?'

'I don't know really. I was about seven. He used to come and see me once or twice a year. He used to take the photo out of his pocket and look at it when mother was out of the room. He had lovely eyes. After I stole the photo I never saw him again. Perhaps he married her. I imagined him with her, with Fiona. Mother was glad to see the back of him. She was going with an insurance salesman from Kentish Town. He was a vulgar little person. I hated him. I imagined my father with Fiona and thought he was better off. Better off without mother. She was a cow.'

'Ah,' said Isobel.

'He's dead now. I never really knew him. He gave us this house. He owned property. Mother didn't like him because he was quiet, quiet and dreamy. She despised him for his generosity. She thought his kindness to her was a sign of weakness. She preferred a good slap. I hope he married Fiona and found happiness. It's strange, you're the image of her.'

'Am I?'

'Don't you think so?'

'I can't really tell. It's difficult to say.'

'Take my word for it. It's uncanny the likeness. I asked my mother about my father before she died but she wouldn't tell me anything. I asked her to tell me what he was like but she said she could hardly remember. "Ships that pass in the night," she said. "A moment of folly." I asked her whether he had married. "I doubt it," she said. "He had a few bob but he was a bit of a goon," she said. "Silly over women, if I recall," she said. "If I recall." She could hardly remember. Those were her last words. And then she passed away.'

'Terrible,' said Isobel. 'It must be terrible not to know your father.'

'You get used to it,' said Sylvia. 'I must get on,' she added.

'I'll be going then. Goodbye.'

'Goodbye dear. Thanks for the flowers. See you soon.'

Isobel ran across the road through the rain and opened the door of the blue house. There was silence as of absence and yet she knew her father was at home. Fiona must be sleeping. Isobel tiptoed into the hall and crept up the stairs.

The door of the nursery was shut. Isobel pressed her ear to it, heard nothing, and opened the door. Her father stood at the head of the cot gazing fondly at the sleeping child.

'What are you doing?' she demanded.

'I am trying to look after this child.'

'Get out of here,' said Isobel.

'Why? Why are you always hissing at me? You're jealous of your own child. Can't you see I'm trying to help?'

'Get out,' Isobel repeated.

'Why?'

'What about me?' said Isobel.

'What about you? You are always screaming at me.'

Isobel screamed at him. 'Why don't you love me?'

'Look what you've done. You've made her cry. I hate you.'

'I hate you. Fuck you. Fuck off.'

'I will. You are a selfish little bitch,' said Antony.

Isobel picked up the wailing child and comforted her until she was sleeping. The baby's breath was milky. Isobel kissed her on the mouth, laid her down in the cot, and began to cry. She leant over the cot and her tears fell on to the face of the sleeping child. 'I'm going to bed,' she said.

Discarded clothes, retaining the shape of limbs they have accommodated, and shoes, animated as if still containing feet, lie on the floor where they have fallen in dust and fluff. A muddled heap of blankets and sheets is humped on the bed like a headless man. It would be unhygienic and uncomfortable to lie under that heap of covers having removed only your shoes and maybe your skirt to prevent it from creasing should you ever feel like getting up again – it would be unhygienic and uncomfortable to lie in bed wearing knickers and tights and bra and shirt and jersey; closely fitting underwear makes marks on your body when you are sleeping; blood burst spots appear under your skin on shoulders where your bra-straps cut and red raw knicker stripes circle round your thighs. Bacteria multiply in the traps of pocketed air incubated by your body heat. The pillow is grey and grubby, spotted with bled mascara from weeping. In the afternoon there is no darkness but shadows. It is a fine time for weeping. The dirty bed is cosy. The clock is ticking into silence. Why am I crying?

I am crying because my father hates me. He hates me with his big brown eyes and his beard and his belly belted underneath with his big brown belt. He hates me with his soft pink hands and his soft red lips. He hates me. That's a fact. I have lost all my tears now. Between sleeping and waking a thickness as of the supple edges of hands and feet and the reflex shrink and wrinkle of eyelid and foreskin make tactile skin-soft pressings on the retina of the mind's eye. Is it a dream or waking sense of flesh? Feet nestle like doves paired in the spring. Hands press palm to palm and edge to edge to open like a book. The stroke of skin on skin is papery. A voice whispers into the waxy orifice of the ear. Breath warms the little lobe. 'Isobel. Isobel.'

The voice slips in like two fingers. Breath warms the neck and breast. This is a dream of inserted pleasure ridden on wanted whispers. The voice penetrates, dissolving tautness in a gush. Eyes and lips open a crack to meet the crack of open eyes and lips. 'Isobel. Isobel.'

Antony is kneeling beside the messed-up bed. His eyes are washed by tears. 'I am sorry. I am sorry.' His touch on her forehead is the caress of dreams.

'Wake me,' she said. 'Wake me.'

'You are not sleeping.'

'This is a dream.'

'No,' said Antony. 'I am sorry.'

Isobel held out her arms to her father. He is humble. He is humble. His brokenness brought no pleasure. He laid his cheek against her chest.

'Don't,' said Isobel. Gently she pushed away his nuzzling head.

'Don't cry. This is not what I want. This is not what I want at all. Talk to me,' she said.

Antony raised himself from his knees and sat down on the edge of the bed. 'My father used to weep,' he said. 'My mother made my father weep.'

'I look like your mother,' said Isobel. 'Fiona.'

'Yes,' said Antony. 'Your mother made me weep.'

'You make me weep,' said Isobel.

It was terrible to see her father crying. His marbled eyes were sluiced and dripping.

'Forgive me,' he said. 'I am crying for my mother and my wife. Why are you crying?'

'I thought you were crying for me,' said Isobel. 'Why don't you love me?'

'I will try,' said Antony. 'I will try.'

'Thank you,' said Isobel. 'Now I must sleep.'

Antony lumbered towards the door.

Sleep annihilated waking pain and immersed Isobel in oblivious darkness. At midnight, eyes swollen, a crust of dry mucus encircling the inside membrane of each nostril, Isobel fell out of bed, got up and stumbled towards the door. She opened it and there on the landing, sitting hunched beside a plastic carrier-bag containing books and papers, was her father, reading a paperback novel, his head resting in his hand.

'Hello Dad,' said Isobel.

'Hello dear. Come and sit down,' said Antony.

Twenty-eight

Mr Green had been a regular church-goer for many years. As a boy, dressed in his Sunday suit of blue serge, he would have found missing the Sunday service inconceivable. His shirt was boiled and starched and ironed until in whiteness it resembled the lilies of the altar, and in stiffness the marble slabs of graves. A short fat tie of knitted wool, brown and blue, blue and brown, made by his mother out of scraps gleaned from the yearly fabrication of his father's winter woolly, was knotted tightly round his neck. His short fair hair was parted on one side and plastered to his scalp with a splash of brilliantine that was perfumed with attar of roses. It was his father's brilliantine. It was his father's ashen rosy smell. His mother smelled of lavender. Martin Green's shoes were polished – the shoe-shine kit hung in a Dorothy bag on a hook on the inside of the laundry door. Sunday morning he polished his shoes and bathed and endured the anxious clucking of his mother's tongue as she smoothed and parted his hair. Yes, it would have been inconceivable for him to miss church.

And yet, since childhood, his attendance had not been constant; there was a gap after the war during which he joined an amateur dramatics society and appeared in a series of radical plays; after performances he would sit up with friends and deprecate vehemently the institutions of church and state; Sunday mornings were spent sleeping off the smoke, wine and jazz of the night before.

However, the blustering and posturing of his young friends began to bore him. As he reached thirty he abandoned them, threw himself into his work, and slipped back into the Sunday routine of his childhood. The church pleased him in its dullness and the meagre singing of the congregation. Sylvia had suggested a registry office wedding.

'I am hardly a virgin,' she said. 'Not to put too fine a point on it,' she added, and laughed.

But Mr Green insisted. He had a word with the vicar. The church is forgiving. The matter was settled.

And so the bells rang, one blue yellow morning in August, and the guests gathered in the sunshine outside St Mary's. The pealing of the bells was jubilant; the guests raised cheerful voices; the walls of the church were cool and grey.

Lily arrived on the good arm of her husband. The empty sleeve of his dark suit was pressed flat and tucked into the pocket of his jacket. The gilt of buttons and ornamental buckles glinted on the front of Lily's dress and coat. Round her neck she wore a sovereign that shone like a medal. Behind her, Mr Elbrooke, magnificent in morning-dress, walked stiffly up the steps of the church and shook hands with the verger. As he mounted, the tails of his coat opened like the grey wings of a bird. You could see the voluminous stripy cloth of his trousers flapping round his knees. Holding the verger's hand gently with the tips of his fat fingers he smiled benignly and indicated with his eyes the scarlet sober face of Seamus who was stepping carefully out of a taxi. The verger withdrew his hand as Seamus waved at his wife, who was waiting for him under a tree. Dolly, Vi and Maureen sat down on a bench and put their heads together for a natter in the churchyard. The pale colours of their dresses were festive, their hats were trimmed with flowers, and their feet were shod in shiny shoes.

'What a little angel,' said Maureen, as Isobel passed pushing Fiona in her pram.

Abruptly the bells stopped ringing. At the church door the vicar bobbed to the wedding guests in his yellowing collar and extended his frail arms. Bending from the waist to reduce his spindly height he greeted members of the congregation. The cloth of his suit was mildewed green and soft with age.

Out of the greyness of the church the organ roared. Young voices lifted in praise. The Lord's my shepherd I'll not want he makes me down to lie. The guests were drawn into the church by the music. There was a silence of reverence as they trod the aisle and breathed the still cold air but as they settled into their seats, adjusted their clothing and made themselves comfortable, the church was full of whispers. It contained the wedding guests only as a cinema contains an audience before the show; the holy aroma of damp and the jewelled light streaming through coloured glass could not quieten the congregation. The pews were hard but there were cushions provided. A crucified Christ was displayed behind the altar but his crown of thorns was fetching, and the blood stuck to his brow and palms like jam. The choir was singing. Goodness and mercy all my days shall surely follow me.

The organist struck an angry chord that thundered through the church and startled the guests into silence. At the church door a shuffling of uncertain feet could be heard as the wedding party arrived. Then it was the Wedding March to welcome the bride. The guests twisted their heads round to watch her advance towards the altar on the arm of Antony Lord. The bride was dressed in plain white silk that covered her from head to toe. Beneath a veil of fine netting her face was obscured. In fact it was impossible to recognise her. Mr Green and Mr Mackenzie, the best-man, followed along behind.

It was difficult to hear the words of the service; the vicar's voice was small and dry. And yet the responses rang out joyfully – I do, I do. Sylvia and Mr Green were married. To kiss the bride it was necessary for Mr Green to search beneath the folds of floating stuff for her mouth. He caught up handfuls of billowing veiling and managed to expose her chin and lips. It was only when her eyes became visible that Norman, who was watching the service dreamily from his pew by the church door, saw clearly that the virginal swathed figure was his mother. The kiss was brief and yet the smack of mouth on mouth sealed the union of his mother with Mr Green and sounded juicily as a reminder of what had gone before between them, and as a prelude to future smackings and suckings and lickings.

'Who can find a virtuous woman?' said the vicar. 'For her price is above rubies.' His small voice lifted, persisted, berated, placated and fell away. The congregation rose noisily to their feet and began to sing. Norman opened his mouth automatically and joined in. We know we at the end shall life inherit. It was Sylvia's favourite. There was a man behind Norman whose voice rose out of the general cheerful drone tunelessly. Then the church doors opened and the wedding guests poured out of the gloom into the sunshine.

Norman blinked. The stripping noon glare was cruel. His mother, her veil thrown back off her face, no longer looked like a bride. Out of the church her head was no longer bent in reverence or uneasiness under the weight of the spirit of God in God's house. Out of the blurring shadows Sylvia grinned and giggled. She looked like Sylvia, Sylvia who had exchanged her drip-dry overall and tan-coloured nylons for the finery of a bride. She was laughing. Until the kiss, her blurred eyes through the veil lied as if she were no longer a mother. To see her lips move. We know we at the end shall life inherit. It was lying. The church made Sylvia unrecognisable. Before the kiss she was a holy virgin bride. She was a childless bride. There is no son of the virgin. And then after the lifting of the veil and the recognition of his mother's eyes – that was the truth – it was Mr and Mrs Green. My mother Mrs Green. I am squeezed out. I am out.

Out on the dry green August grass his mother was laughing and holding hands with Mr Green. She hitched up the long skirts of her wedding dress to stop it from trailing in the dust and laughed. The guests were gathering behind her for the photographs. Mr Green was shouting. Norman saw the deep cave of darkness inside his mouth – inside it was red and black like hell.

'Norman,' he shouted. 'The photographs. Come on.'

Sylvia stood between her husband and her son for the group picture. Isobel stood beside Norman, and Antony stood beside Mr Green. Little Fiona sat on a folded blanket at Sylvia's feet. The photographer waved his hand at the baby and clicked his tongue against the roof of his mouth in imitation of a horse trotting to draw the child's attention to the camera and make her smile. Fiona smiled. The shutter of the camera clicked. On tip-toe the guests peered over the heads of the family party to get a look in. The shutter clicked. The photographer rearranged the group so that Sylvia was flanked by Antony and Mr Green. Isobel took her place beside her father with Fiona in her arms. Norman appeared from behind his mother and stood next to Isobel but the photographer moved him, for the sake of symmetry, to the side of Mr Green.

'Where are the bridesmaids?' asked the photographer.

'We decided against them,' said Mr Green.

Again the shutter clicked. Again the group was broken up and rearranged. Confetti littered the dusty grass. Maureen and Dolly and Vi approached the bride and groom to offer congratulations. There was much kissing and handshaking. The shutter clicked.

Norman was unable to remain among the joyful crowd. He sidled away into the shadows behind the church and leant his forehead against the cold stone of a streaked buttress rising like a tree trunk out of the earth. The buttress exuded the mouldy smell of the grave. The earth was black and rich with goodness that seeped out of corpses. Now Sylvia and Mr Green would be embracing at the church door. The embrace would be empty – there was no nature in it – it was made for the photographer. Thankfully. The real dirty lusty juicy stuff would come later. Sylvia and Mr Green would be sealed together under the pale candlewick bedspread of Sylvia's bed and Norman would be squeezed out. He would lie in his own bed and hold his breath and listen. He would listen to their sighs and groans. And then when the mounting lisped cries of love overcame him he would bury his head beneath the blankets and pretend that he was dead.

Voices could be heard clearly now. Norman lifted his forehead off the buttress and listened. It was Isobel and Antony and Fiona taking a stroll beside the church. Antony's voice was deep, caressing. 'You look marvellous in that dress,' he said.

Isobel laughed shyly and thanked him.

'I am proud of you,' he said.

Fiona was babbling and giggling and calling out to Isobel. 'Mum mum mum mum mum.'

Norman heard Isobel's fond endearments.

'Isn't she lovely,' said Antony. 'You are a clever girl.'

Isobel and Antony would be embracing beside the church in happiness. His beard would brush her soft cheek and his chubby arms would fold her to his chest, his thighs, his loins. Norman was squeezed out. He heard Isobel sighing, or the rub of leaf on leaf in the trees. Was that Fiona giggling or birdsong? He heard mischievous laughter and leapt out from behind the church.

'Why are you laughing?' he demanded. 'Are you laughing at me?'

146

'No,' said Isobel. 'Don't be silly. We are laughing at your mother.'

Norman looked into Isobel's blissful face and ran away across the ancient gravestones into the bushes.

The reception was held in the church hall, a solid red brick building erected across the road from the church for celebrations and social functions after the war.

The guests, leaving the churchyard, carried with them the gaiety of the marriage into the street and gathered on the pavement in their wedding clothes, waiting for a gap in the traffic to cross the road. In their pride and cheerful awkward self-importance they made big gestures and looked at the traffic as if it might stop ceremoniously in deference to them. The driver of a passing car honked in acknowledgement of the occasion or to warn them to keep out of his way.

'Cheeky bastard,' said Lily, adjusting the angle of her hat.

Passers-by collected on the other side of the road to watch the splendid mob spilling out of the church gates and crowding the pavement. The watchers were waiting for a glimpse of the bride. At last there was a break in the queue of cars. Sylvia and Mr Green moved through the parting crowd and led the guests across the road.

The doorway of the hall was hung with garlands and ribbons. Mrs Mackenzie, making a final adjustment to the foliage and flowers, removed her apron as the bride and groom entered, shoved it into her handbag and stood to one side. Music crackled and boomed out of loudspeakers perched in the corners of the hall above head-height on little triangular brackets. Sylvia gasped.

The hall was beautiful. An expanse of polished parquet, dark and luminous, stretched like a sheet of still water in sunshine to the far wall where, draped with heavy linen cloths, the buffet tables were laid. Black-eyed tulips, scarlet and white, their leaves drooping gracefully, brimmed out of glass vases and scattered pollen on to the cloths. Heaps of polished fruits, their burnished skin like

jewels, flamed in abundance on platters of silver. Dainty
sandwiches, trimmed and crustless, the bread kept moist
by tin-foil and napkins, were revealed by Mrs Mackenzie as
she saw to the removal of the covers as the guests arrived.
There was cold chicken, ready carved, glazed and sprinkled
with parsley, sausages on sticks, salad, and veal and ham
pie. In cut-glass bowls the trifle was layered, cream on
custard on jelly and sponge. The surface was sprinkled
with sugar strands. Bread rolls, white and brown, seeded
and plain, lay in baskets lined with doilies, and the butter,
arranged on little plates decorated with mustard and cress,
was curled and iced. Large dinner plates, in readiness for
the onslaught of the guests, were stacked on a card table to
one side of the buffet; and, beside the plates, the cutlery
was set out in numerous small bundles, one for each guest,
three pieces folded in a napkin, red or white – knife, fork
and spoon. At the other end of the buffet, on a table of its
own, the wedding cake stood, three-tiered and pillared and
pedimental like a Greek temple; the icing was smooth and
hard as plaster; two figures stood on the top like gods.

'It's beautiful,' said Sylvia.

She thanked Mrs Mackenzie for all her help. The hall
was filling up with guests who took seats in rows around
the walls or gathered at the makeshift bar where Eric from
The George was serving drinks. Mr Green, a pint glass in
his hand, his tie undone and dangling, the collar of his shirt
unbuttoned, a patchy flush speckling his neck and cheeks
and browbone, stood by the door of the gents with Mr
Mackenzie and Mr Elbrooke and made them laugh.

'At my age,' he said. 'I can hardly believe it.'

'It's never too late,' said Mr Elbrooke.

'So they say. So they say.'

Mr Mackenzie pushed his florid face forward and whispered into Mr Green's ear.

'I should say so,' said Mr Green. 'No worries in that
department.' He raised his glass to his lips deliberately and
took a long gulp. Above the thick bottom of his glass his

eyebrows rose and fell comically. His companions laughed at his winking and smirking and nudged him in the ribs with their elbows like schoolboys. Mr Green, tickled by the hilarity he had induced, made an effort not to choke on his beer. At that moment Norman appeared, immaculate in a pale grey suit, his face composed and sober.

'Woof woof,' he said, in passing, and moved away into the lavatory. Mr Mackenzie and Mr Elbrooke exchanged bemused and kindly glances. Mr Green swallowed and buttoned-up the collar of his shirt.

'I think Norman is a little upset,' he said.

'It's only natural,' said Mr Mackenzie.

'He'll get over it,' said Mr Elbrooke. 'Never mind,' he added.

'Anyone for another?' said Mr Green, raising his empty glass.

He led his friends away quickly from the door of the gents to avoid another brush with Norman, and made for the bar.

'Poor sod,' he said.

It was a slow dance that drew the first couples on to the dance floor. The music swelled out of the loudspeakers, plucked notes bleating, and the heave of a heartfelt voice moved the wedding guests to their feet. The singer's voice was know-all and injured. Lily's husband held his wife firmly round the waist with his good arm and counted.

'One two three four. One two three four.'

He counted until they were caught by the rhythm. They swayed together from side to side and shuffled their feet. Maureen and Vi were dancing together. Maureen's dress was mauve on lilac. Vi's dress was pink on mauve. They held their handbags in the angles of their elbows, and held each other lightly. Mr Elbrooke cut in and left Vi alone on the floor. She was jigging without a partner. The movements of her arms became jerky and she shrugged her shoulders. Mrs Mackenzie rescued her by waving from the buffet with both arms above her head. Vi walked away quickly from the couples embracing on the floor and joined Mrs Mackenzie in an inspection of the cake. A sob or sigh was caught in the voice of the singer pouring out of the loudspeakers. And if you love him, oh be proud of him, cos after all he's just a man. Tum ti tum ti tum. The song moved round after the chorus and returned to the beginning. You have good times, you have bad times, doing things you don't understand. But if you love him, you'll forgive him, even though he's hard to understand. Lily felt the forearm of her husband firm against the small of her back. They swayed together and shuffled their feet. The singer was pleading. Oh be proud of him.

Seamus took to the floor with his wife, stepping carefully to avoid treading on her feet; in his big fist he held her small hand; she rested her cheek against his chest. As the dance progressed he extended his own arm so that her arm was almost unbent with the distance. He swung her round and round. There was almost a collision. It was Eric in the way, feigning reluctance to dance and struggling in the arms of the barmaid from The George. Seamus managed to sidestep the clumsy couple without upsetting his wife who was lost in the dance.

Children in their best clothes skipped and ran between the dancers, the little girls holding out the hems of their dresses daintily, the little boys smirking and chasing rowdily through the pairs of swaying adults as if excited or embarrassed by the closeness and the music. Dolly's grandchildren, a couple of timid boys in velour tracksuits, stood side by side by the buffet and watched their grandmother lift her skirts and circle round their grandfather, her face flushed.

Norman was dancing with his mother. The skirt of her wedding dress was trailing on the floor. A film of beady moisture caught in the pores of Norman's upper lip and his eyes were closed. The song ended with a long drawn out note of resignation, a dragged out one more time note of reiteration prolonged to give the dancers a few last seconds in each other's arms. Norman was still holding on to his mother in the silence after the last chord. It was as if he were unable to disentangle himself from the embrace.

'Norman,' she said. 'Let go of me son.'

Norman let go of her suddenly and opened his eyes. 'Sorry, mother,' he said, blinking and squinting into her face. 'I was deep in thought.'

'Are you all right?' Sylvia asked him.

'Here comes Mr Green,' said Norman.

Sylvia turned and saw that her husband was hurrying towards her across the gleaming floor of the hall.

'Don't call him Mr Green,' said Sylvia. 'You know his name.'

But Norman was not listening to her. He was loping away towards the lavatories with the knuckle of his forefinger jammed in his mouth.

'Shall we dance?' said Mr Green.

As the bride and groom danced, the guests, emboldened by drinking and the example of Isobel and Antony, who were feeding sandwiches to Fiona, gathered round the buffet and loaded their plates. Then it was time to cut the cake. Mrs Mackenzie dismantled the tiers and laid the little plaster pillars to one side. She wrapped the miniature plastic bridal pair in a paper napkin and put it in her handbag for safe keeping until later when she would present it to Sylvia as a souvenir. Sylvia took the long knife in both hands and closed her eyes, summoning up in her head a formulation for the hazy wordless hopefulness brought on by the wedding and the wine. It was strange to summon words for a wish that would never be uttered. And yet words were necessary. Without words the wish would not exist. She already had everything she could wish for. The wish then would be for Norman. Poor Norman. The wish was I love Norman. Poor Norman. Happiness for Norman. That was it. Mr Green enfolded her hands in his. Together they cut the cake.

'Did you wish?' asked Mr Green.

'Of course,' said Sylvia.

The guests were clapping and cheering and holding out small plates to receive the cake Mrs Mackenzie was cutting into little cubes. The cake was dark under the bright yellow marzipan and the whiteness of the icing. Isobel broke off a small piece and popped it into Fiona's mouth. Eric folded a slice in his handkerchief to take home to his old mother. Out of the loudspeakers it was Tie a yellow ribbon round the old oak tree.

Norman was singing along, grinning and slapping his thighs. 'I like this one,' he said, looking at Isobel. 'Please dance with me.'

Isobel left Fiona with her father and followed Norman on to the middle of the floor.

'Are you all right Norman?' she asked. 'You look a bit odd.'

'As well as can be expected,' he replied, swinging his arms widely in time to the music. 'Why weren't you the bridesmaid?'

'I don't believe in marriage,' she answered. 'It's stupid.'

'Don't you want to get married?'

'No. Never. I have other plans.'

'I have plans too,' said Norman. 'You wait and see.'

And with that he began to whistle.

Now that the guests were sitting down the hall looked a little empty.

'Lovely cake,' said Lily. 'You see her, on the floor with Norman? Well that's the mother of his little one.'

'So young looking,' said Maureen.

'So young,' said Vi.

'And that's the father. Him with the beard.'

'Oh,' said Dolly.

'Yes,' said Vi.

'He's a distant relation of Sylv's apparently.'

'They met at a funeral,' said Lily. 'She told me. It was a second cousin or something, the deceased.'

'She told me all about it. Relations, and neighbours, she said.'

'Nice,' said Vi.

'The baby's a little beauty,' said Lily.

Fiona was holding her grubby little face up obediently to be wiped with the corner of Antony's handkerchief. Once her face was clean she toddled off to play with some other small children who had made a camp under one of the buffet tables. Her chubby little legs were sturdy and firm.

'Be good,' said Antony as she disappeared beneath the canopy of white linen.

The song faded away. Norman bowed to Isobel.

'Time to go home,' she said. 'I don't want Fiona to get tired.'

'Mr Green has bought a car,' said Norman. 'He said I can borrow it whenever I like.'

'How nice,' said Isobel. 'We are going to the clinic on Saturday,' she added. 'You can give us a lift.'

'Fine,' said Norman.

'Goodbye. See you then.'

'I'll fetch Fiona,' said Antony.

He found her under the table squeezed in the thin arms of a white-faced child.

'Come on darling,' he said.

Fiona held out her arms to him.

'Time to go home.'

Norman watched Antony and Isobel as between them they led Fiona to the door. He saw them kiss his mother and shake hands with Mr Green.

'Come on darlings,' said Antony, holding open the door.

Mr Green closed the door behind them and turned to face Sylvia. He took her hands in his and kissed her on the neck where the skin was moist and powdered. He went nuzzling into her neck with puckered lips. There was a ringed hand stroking the bristled skin of his scalp, a homely mottled hand protruding from the slim white sleeve of the wedding dress. She must have disengaged her hand from

the hand of Mr Green. She must have tugged slightly until
he had released the pressure of his gripping fingers on her
palm and then pulled her hand away. The withdrawal of
her hand, tactful yet firm, did it hurt? Did the hand of
Mr Green feel empty? Did Mr Green feel empty in the
instant before the withdrawn hand landed on his head?
He brushed her earlobe with his lips. He opened his lips
and licked her earlobe with the tip of his tongue. With
his empty hand he cupped her breast upholstered in white
satin and tweaked the point at the end of the dart behind
which the nipple hardened. Stooping to grasp the fabric
of her skirts and petticoats he hoisted it above her knee
and inserted his hand between her thighs. The rubbing of
his palm on her skin made a papery noise. His hand rose
higher and higher towards the gusset of her knickers above
her stocking tops under cover of the curtain of white satin.
The elastic of her knickers was tight around her thighs. He
eased one finger inside the elastic. The finger wormed its
way through a tangle of coarse hair and waggled inside the
hairy crack. The membranes were slippery inside the hairy
dryness of the lips. Mr Green slipped his finger inside her
and rubbed and rubbed. His mouth was open against her
open mouth. He licked her teeth and gums. She unbuttoned
the flies of his wedding trousers and took his fat penis in her
hand. Kneeling as if to retrieve a dropped handkerchief she
pushed her face against his crotch and swiftly touched his
penis with her tongue. She felt empty without his finger
inside her. Her vagina was gaping. His penis was enormous.
When she rose she left her knickers behind her on the floor
of the church hall. Neatly she flicked them under a table
with the toe of her shoe. Manoeuvring round so that her
back was against the wall beside the door to the lavatories
she opened her arms to Mr Green. He pressed himself
against her with his back to the wedding guests and again
scooped up her skirts. The folds and gathers fell in swathes
over her thighs. She opened her legs slightly. Releasing his
penis from inside his trousers Mr Green guided it with

his hand into his wife's vagina. Behind him the tails of his morning-coat were dangling. He stood on tip-toe and groaned.

Twenty-nine

The interior of Mr Green's car was compact and somewhat dusty; the seats, upholstered in beige brushed nylon, were a little worn; he had bought it, second-hand, from a friend. Norman held the steering-wheel in his left hand, his fingers loosely folded round the thonged leather steering wheel cover, and put his foot down. His right elbow, resting on the rubberised sill, stuck out of the open window into the sunshine. His blue blue eyes, cornflower blue, set in pools of whiteness traced with blue-red veins, peered, between thick lids stuck with silver stubble lashes, at the road. He glanced into the rear-view mirror, saw the top of Isobel's golden head, and looked again at the road. The road was clear in front and behind. Parked cars lined the street on either side, leaving only a narrow strip down which to drive.

'Don't go too fast,' said Isobel. 'It's dangerous.'

Fiona began to babble. 'Mum mum mum mum. Da da da da da.'

Norman said nothing. The speed of the car remained constant.

The tarmac tainted breeze, a breath redolent of green leaves, subtle and spoiled, particled and sparkling, made

Norman blink – his lowered lid scraped grit across his eye. Through the glass of the windscreen a refracted greenhouse warmth lifted Isobel's closed eyes to the sun. In her arms, bared for the summer and faintly downy, she held Fiona, stilled by the heat.

Trees cast dappled shadows over parked cars and pavements. Pedestrians, divested of their overcoats, in cool summer outfits, or caught out by the sunshine in dismal woollies, moved in and out of the patches of sunlight and shadow. The palings of fences flickered and the wing-mirrors of parked cars flashed.

Isobel turned her head languidly, brushing the hair from her brow with her hand. Slowly she lifted her eyelids; light and greenness seeped into her eyes. They were speeding past the railwayland.

'Look,' said Isobel. 'Look Fiona.'

Behind the fence a silver train slipped away beyond the allotments.

'Look, a train,' said Isobel.

'Train,' Fiona repeated.

White flowered nettles, fleshy and bristle-haired, and the veined leaves of dock, and cow parsley, a cloud of tiny creamy flowers, and the Indian pink-eyed campion, staring out of the tangle of leaf and stalk, pressed against the ramshackle fencing of chicken-wire, palings and railings as if to escape. Tender new shoots poked out of holes in wire netting and above, scaling the palings abundantly, the trembling shock of bramble and bindweed spilled over out of the railwayland into the street.

Fiona was not looking out of the window. She gazed up into the face of her mother, into her mother's eyes that were focused elsewhere, and curled her fist around her mother's thumb. 'Mum mum mum,' she said, squirming to rise in Isobel's lap. In the staring disks of her mother's eyes the green of the tumbling verdure was reflected. The sky was reflected. A white cloud was floating in her eye.

'Mum mum mum,' said Fiona, calling Isobel back from

strangeness. Her mother's eyes returned and she saw her own image trapped inside them. Looking into her mother's eyes she saw herself and smiled.

Then they passed the corner shop. There was a squeal of brakes. Norman stuck his head and shoulders out of the window. 'You silly bastard,' he shouted.

A large black car was roaring away into the distance.

'You stupid cunt,' he shouted.

'Don't swear,' said Isobel. 'I don't want her to pick up your nonsense.'

Norman said nothing. A large tear swelled in the eye of the child and fell.

'It's all right, darling, don't be scared of Norman,' said Isobel.

Fiona's tiny eyebrows were lifted and puckered in fright.

'Come on darling, there's a good girl.'

'Mum mum mum,' said Fiona and opened her moist red mouth.

The buttons that fastened the front of Isobel's dress were large and smooth like flying saucers. Fiona stuck out a finger and prodded them one by one.

'Un two two five,' she said.

'One two three four five,' said Isobel.

Fiona gasped and wailed with laughter. 'Un un un five,' she shrieked, bouncing on Isobel's lap. 'Un un un five,' she whispered, her eyes saucy with excitement as she fingered the buttons of Isobel's dress. She touched the buttons gingerly as if they might bite and looked into her mother's face and howled.

Norman glanced into the rear-view mirror and saw the parked cars streaming away behind him into the clear blue brightness of the sky. Framed in the small mirror Isobel's fine mouth was fixed with a faint smile. It was a smile of patience. And yet her eyes were blue and amused. Her eyes were proud.

'Say hello to Daddy,' said Norman.

'Da da,' the child replied.

They were nearly home. It was Mr Green's slippers now that lay together nose to nose and furry like a pair of little dogs in front of the fire. It was what would you like for dinner Martin, stick your dick up my cunt Martin, shall we go to bingo Martin, ta ta Norman, now.

There was Mr Green leading Sylvia along the pavement in front of the blue house dressed up for the summer in a lightweight jacket and a cravat of periwinkle blue. Sylvia skipped girlishly behind him, her hand in his, the pale skirt of her dress billowing, showing her strong legs. As they stepped off the pavement into the road they turned their smiling summer faces towards the advancing car and waved. Norman caught their smiles stretch into laughter and shrink as he put his foot down. Mr Green was standing in the middle of the road with his mouth open. It was Mr Green he was aiming for but Sylvia leapt to save him and Norman knocked her down. There was a dull thud. Impact sent the body grazing across tarmac to stillness. Isobel covered Fiona's eyes.

Sylvia's eyes were closed. Her head lolled as if unhinged, dragging the brown folds of her neck apart with its weight to show inside creases the tender pink of untanned skin. The waxen earlobes gashed with stretched and empty piercings looked so delicate. Parted and drawn her faded hair was combed behind her ears. The parting that bisected her skull was scaly and scalp blue. Her mouth was open. In the sunshine you could see the crazed blackness of her back teeth and the little gleaming epiglottis. Attached yet unsocketed her flung limbs turned their pale and veined undersides to the sky. Her right foot was twisted on the tarmac. It was her shell-pink lock-knit knickers that made her thighs look so white. I can't remember whether it was a voice scraping out of her throat first or her eyes opening. Anyhow, it was just a slit that appeared in the smear of blue eye-shadow and her voice was no more than a whisper. 'Norman,' she whispered.

The kneeling figure of Mr Green rose to make way for her son.

Norman was leaning against the hot and polished wing of a parked car. He saw Mr Green rise from his mother's side and hurry towards the blue house. His mother's lips were moving. 'Norman,' she murmured.

His mother was smiling. The whites of her eyes gleamed in slitted lids. The pupils had turned away into the back of her head. 'Norman,' she repeated.

Norman lowered his own body on to the body of his mother, taking the weight on his muscular sun-tanned arms. Her belly undulated softly under the hardness of his. There was an angularity and jolting of bones inside the softness of his mother's flesh and yet she was mainly softness. Her breasts made a firm and yielding cushion for his chest.

'Hold me,' he said. 'Hold me.'

He placed his mouth on her mouth and knew that she was no longer breathing.

A crowd gathered above the bodies of Norman and Sylvia. A siren was wailing. Mr Green was talking to a policeman.

'It was my wife,' he said. 'We were having an argument. She ran out into the road.'

Antony came out of the blue house to fetch his daughter and her child. Norman ran away into the railwayland.